"A touching love story with a paranormal twist is what I found within the pages of this book...Deanna Kahler takes Celeste on an eye-opening journey, and the reader goes along as well."
~ *Brenda Casto for Readers' Favorite*

"*Echoes of Paradise* is powerful, inspirational, and filled with spiritual reflection."
~ *Diane Donovan, Senior eBook Reviewer, Midwest Book Review*

"A pleasing spiritual romance about love lost and regained."
~ *Kirkus Reviews*

"This is a beautiful story about not just the eternal love between two soul mates, but also the universal love that really is all there is."
~ *Roberta Grimes, attorney, author and afterlife researcher*

"*Echoes of Paradise* is a sweet tale with a metaphysical slant about spiritual growth and enlightenment... I recommend this book for romance fans, especially those who enjoy stories about loving ghosts, life beyond death, metaphysics or parables of enlightenment such as *The Celestine Prophecy.*"
~ *Deb Sanders, author*

Echoes of Paradise

by Deanna Kahler

ISBN-10: 0615863396
ISBN-13: 978-0615863399

Library of Congress Control Number: 2013918717

Published by Rose Petal Publications
Shelby Township, MI

Printed in the United States of America
Second Edition, May 2016

DEDICATION

I dedicate this book to all those who have touched my life and left this world. Thank you for inspiring me and helping me to believe in something more.

"Of course you don't die. Nobody dies.
Death doesn't exist. You only reach a new
level of vision, a new realm of consciousness,
a new unknown world."

~ Henry Miller

CONTENTS

CONTENTS (continued)

PREFACE

M ost of us have experienced something unusual that we couldn't explain. You think of your deceased grandmother, and her picture falls off the mantle. You have a very vivid dream of your mom in spirit and wake up feeling like you actually spent time with her. You think of your brother who passed and immediately hear a song that reminds you of him. These are just a few of the mysterious occurrences many people encounter. When these events happen, we may wonder: Can the deceased see and hear us? Do they visit us sometimes? But often we dismiss our experiences as just imagination or pure coincidence. After all, how can we believe in something we can't explain?

This book explores the mysterious happenings in our lives and the phenomenon of spirit communication. It delves into the world beyond and our connections with others. It invites you to *consider the possibilities*.

Although the story is fiction, it was inspired by the unusual real-life experiences that many people have. I must admit, I have had several myself, some of which are included in this book. While these occurrences are difficult to comprehend, they often leave us with a sense of being part of something greater than ourselves. These unexpected events uplift us and encourage us to look beyond the physical world and be aware of all that is around us.

As you read through the pages of this book, I hope you'll find the story entertaining, touching, captivating, and inspiring—whether you believe in these types of experiences or not.

No one knows for sure exactly what happens after we die. I can't convince you to believe or not believe in something—that's up to you to decide. But I can tell you this: when you open your mind and heart to the possibilities, sometimes miracles can occur. I've witnessed these miracles, and although I can't fully explain them, I know without a doubt that there is way more to life than meets the eye.

CHAPTER 1
GONE BUT NOT FORGOTTEN

*C*eleste drove down the heavily treed winding road on her way to Marshall's grocery store. She absentmindedly brushed a strand of her wavy golden hair back behind her ear and sighed. It was a crisp October morning, and the leaves on the trees were rich shades of amber, burnt orange, and crimson. The sunlight illuminated the landscape, creating a picture-perfect scene. It was the type of day when onlookers would stop to admire the radiant beauty of the fall season. But not Celeste. She hardly even noticed where she was. She drove mechanically ahead, never pausing to gaze at her surroundings. Her head felt foggy, and her heart ached. There was a heavy, uneasy feeling weighing down on her, holding her body tight like a prisoner in iron chains. As she turned the corner, she began sobbing. Celeste couldn't believe Connor was really gone. This

3

couldn't be happening.

Not him, she thought. *Anyone but Connor*.

He was the one she had held in her heart for so long. He was the one who had saved her from her troubled past and helped heal the painful scars left behind from her abusive ex-boyfriend. Connor was her one true love. Although she had let him go and eventually married someone else, she would never love anyone as completely and deeply as him. She had always hoped that somehow…some way…someday…they would be together again. That was impossible now. He was gone for good. Connor was dead. Nothing and no one could ever bring him back. Any chance they ever had to be together again had died right along with him.

Connor wasn't supposed to die! Not yet anyway. He was far too young—just thirty-five years old. His whole life was still strung out before him, a life that could have included Celeste if only they'd had another chance. That opportunity had now been cruelly and abruptly taken away from them.

Celeste had been looking forward to finally seeing Connor again soon. He had been teaching in Rome since college but had decided it was time to return home. Although he had always been adventurous and had enjoyed exploring a new land and culture, he missed his friends and family. However, he never had the opportunity to see his loved ones again. In a tragic twist of fate, the plane Connor was traveling home on crashed before it reached its destination. No one understood how or why this could have happened, least of all Celeste. All she knew was that her dreams had been shattered and replaced with a trail of emptiness and sorrow. Celeste was feeling her grief profoundly now—so profoundly, in fact, that her mind had begun to play tricks on her.

At times, she swore she had heard Connor's voice whispering in her ear. *It's okay, Celeste. I'm still here.* On other days, she thought she had caught a glimpse of him out of the corner of her eye. As a rational, intelligent woman, she knew that it was all just her imagination. So she chose to ignore what she was experiencing. She had already lost Connor, and she certainly wasn't about to allow herself to lose her sanity too.

It was understandable that Celeste was feeling the way she was. She had gotten her hopes up, only to have them come crashing down like the aircraft that had once carried her lost love. She couldn't help but think about what could have been.

When Celeste found out Connor was moving back, she had felt a surge of excitement. He had left a message on her cell phone that he would be arriving home soon and wanted to see her when he returned. It had been so long, and she couldn't wait to reconnect with him. She pictured his beautiful, charming smile and warm brown eyes. She could feel his strong arms holding her, protecting her. She remembered his playful sense of humor and the way he used to tease her. He loved to be chased and would sometimes run away and make her catch him. But despite his frolicsome nature, he wasn't immature, irresponsible, or weak by any means. He was hardworking, self-sufficient, and intelligent. He knew how to take care of himself and rarely depended on anyone for anything. In relationships, Connor was quiet, strong, and stoic. That didn't mean that he was unemotional or incapable of affection. It was simply the image he projected. He didn't talk openly about his feelings and preferred to keep his innermost thoughts to himself. But Celeste could feel his love and tenderness when they were together. And she always knew she was safe with him.

If she had a problem, Connor was the first person to come to her aid. When her jealous ex-boyfriend, Andy, had keyed her brand-new Mustang, Connor offered to confront him. Although Celeste refused, she appreciated his caring nature and his desire to stand up for her. Connor disliked injustice and wasn't afraid to voice his opinion about anything that wasn't right. She needed someone like him by her side.

But unfortunately, their relationship as a couple didn't last. They had a strong attraction and got along well, but they had different goals and aspirations. Celeste liked stability in her life. She wanted to get married, settle down, and raise a family. She wanted a man who needed her, someone she could take care of.

Connor wasn't that man. He was patient, kind, passionate, and supportive. But he didn't want or need a woman to take care of him. He was too independent and self-sufficient—a bit of a free spirit. Being tied down just didn't suit him. Connor wanted to explore and embrace life. She knew he dreamed of relocating to a foreign country after graduation. He craved adventure and new experiences, while Celeste felt safer with her predictable life and familiar, comfortable surroundings. She had no desire to move anywhere, and certainly not halfway across the world. As much as she longed to be with him, she hadn't wanted to hold him back. And she certainly didn't want to wait around for him to decide if he was ready or willing to settle down. What if he was never ready? It wouldn't be fair to either of them to sacrifice their dreams for each other. So she made the difficult decision to let him go. They parted on good terms, and she never stopped caring about him. Shortly after they split up, Connor set off on a new adventure. He moved to Italy, and she never saw him again.

Celeste did the only thing she could do at the time: she moved on with her life. She finished college and landed a great job as an accountant. She met a wonderful man and got married. And she had a terrific little five-year-old boy named Chip. He was her north star, always asking questions, keeping her on her toes, and displaying the wisdom of a sage. Unfortunately, the marriage was not a source of happiness or fulfillment for Celeste. She and her husband, Dave, had drifted apart over the years and were now separated. They were working hard to overcome their differences through couples therapy, but it was still unclear if they would reconcile or not. Their relationship issues stemmed in part from the fact that Celeste was still in love with Connor.

Throughout her marriage to Dave, Celeste would still sometimes think of Connor and wonder how he was doing. She had always hoped that one day their paths would cross again. She had never wanted him completely out of her life. She just didn't think their relationship would work long term. She had called it off with him to protect herself from future heartbreak and give him the freedom to discover what he wanted in life. She had never been angry or bitter that their relationship didn't work out. Instead, she was left with a sad longing. Although she had no expectation of them becoming a couple again, she had secretly hoped that one day, he would tire of the single life and figure out that all he really wanted and needed was her. Connor was a good person. He was someone she would never forget, no matter how hard she tried. Not even after death.

As Celeste pulled into the crowded grocery store parking lot, the tune "Kiss from a Rose" began playing on her radio. The song was about a man's dead girlfriend and the reminders he had of her. She had always thought the song very sweet and touching, but today, it was a painful reminder of recent events. Connor was dead. He wasn't ever coming back. She would never again see his smiling face or hear his voice. She would never get the chance to tell him how she really felt about him. She would never again feel his strong arms around her or feel his lips kiss her tenderly, yet passionately. She would never get to say good-bye.

"Oh, great," she said sarcastically. "A song about a dead person. Just what I need today!"

She abruptly shut the car off and stormed into the grocery store. Celeste didn't feel like shopping, but staying at home moping wouldn't do her any good. So she got a shopping cart and forced herself to maneuver through the aisles of food, grabbing items she would need to make dinner. As she trudged by the meat counter, filet mignon caught her eye, and she began to think of Connor again.

Celeste remembered how they had met. Her friend Sue had called her and excitedly announced that Bill, a cute guy she had a crush on, had invited her over for dinner. "And he wants me to bring you to meet his friend!" she said enthusiastically.

"Oh, no. I don't do blind dates," Celeste said firmly. She wasn't at all interested in joining them.

"Come on," said Sue encouragingly. "It's just dinner. And besides, I'll be there. It's not like you'd be meeting this guy alone. It will be fine."

Sue was a bit wild and promiscuous—and a master seductress. Getting a guy interested in her was never hard. Sue was absolutely gorgeous, with long, sleek brown hair and eyes the color of emeralds. She wouldn't think twice about a blind date or a one-night stand with some gorgeous guy she met in a bar. She loved to live on the edge and take risks. Spontaneity was her way. Celeste, on the other hand, was more cautious, reserved, and morally sound. She was always the sensible one.

After more begging and pleading, Sue had finally convinced Celeste that the dinner wouldn't be a big deal, and Celeste reluctantly agreed to join them. She wasn't expecting much and was certain "her" guy would turn out to be a creep or a loser. He could just be looking to get laid. Either that or he was a homely, desperate guy who couldn't get a date on his own and needed his friend to help him.

After her last relationship, Celeste wasn't too eager to let a man into her life for fear of getting hurt again. Her ex-boyfriend, Andy, had been a very controlling person who treated her like his possession instead of his girlfriend. He had slapped her, criticized her constantly, and had even pushed her down the stairs one time, breaking her arm. After that horrid experience, she had vowed to never let another man hurt her again. She was guarded and prepared for her meeting with Connor. This time, she was in control. A thick brick wall she had constructed in her mind would keep anyone from getting too close to her.

When Celeste arrived at dinner that night and met Connor for the first time, she was pleasantly surprised. Instead of the homely creep she had envisioned, the person looking back at her was handsome, charming, sexy…and seemed *nice*. He had a medium build and was about five foot eleven. Celeste was immediately drawn to his warm, brown eyes and thick, wavy chestnut hair that made you want to run your fingers through it. When he smiled, he revealed his perfectly straight, dazzling white teeth.

Celeste smiled to herself and thought, *Wow, he's good-looking! I'm sure glad I came.* Of course, his attractiveness didn't guarantee she would like his personality, but it was certainly a start!

The guys had prepared a candlelight dinner for Sue and Celeste, and the table was set nicely. Celeste was surprised and impressed. She had expected something more casual, like burgers and beer. Instead they had created a warm, cozy, romantic atmosphere. Their meal was filet mignon with shallot cream sauce, twice-baked potatoes, asparagus, and red wine. Bill confessed that Connor had done all the cooking, because he didn't know how. Once again, Celeste was impressed.

He's hot—and he can cook, she thought. *I wonder if he's actually nice, too…*

Celeste comfortably settled into her chair at the dining room table and allowed the guys to serve her dinner. It felt good to be pampered, and she found herself enjoying both the food and the company. She was usually quite nervous around guys she didn't know, but for some reason, she felt comfortable and at ease with Connor right away. He quickly proved to be genuinely nice, charming, and intelligent. Celeste remembered that during their meal, Connor sang the Eagles' "Hotel California." Their eyes met, and instead of just gazing in her direction like most guys would, he looked deep into her eyes and touched her soul. He then flashed her a dazzling smile, and she couldn't help but smile back.

Celeste and Connor seemed to hit it off right away. They spent the evening exchanging flirty smiles and making eye contact. Connor was eager to get to know Celeste and asked her questions about what she liked and didn't like. She remembered him asking what kind of music she listened to.

"Do you like Pink Floyd?" he had asked.

"No," she replied.

"Oh, I love Pink Floyd!" he exclaimed. "Are you sure you don't like Pink Floyd?" he asked again with a smirk.

"No...sorry." Celeste smiled flirtatiously.

He seemed disappointed but didn't hold it against her. That was just one thing they didn't agree on.

Sometime later Celeste developed a headache. Connor offered her another glass of wine, but she refused, telling him about her headache.

"You just need to drink more wine!" he responded.

And he again flashed her that sexy, charming smile, his perfect white teeth gleaming in the candlelight. She still politely refused, thinking, *Is this guy trying to get me drunk?*

She wondered if he was hoping to take advantage of

her or if he was just trying to have a good time. She didn't know him well enough to make that determination. But she did know that she was both impressed and intrigued by him. She thoroughly enjoyed the evening and honestly couldn't have asked for a better blind date.

A couple of days later, Sue called.

"Celeste," she said, "Bill wants me to come over, and Connor is going to be there, too. Apparently, Connor was very impressed the other night. He wants to see you again!"

Her heart leapt. This time she excitedly agreed, eager to see Connor again. After their blind date the other night, the brick wall she had constructed to protect herself had begun to crumble.

When Sue and Celeste arrived at Bill's house that evening, Connor surprised Celeste once again. He handed her a beautiful bouquet of red roses. Her heart melted. She thought that was so sweet of him, especially since he had just met her days before. Celeste and Connor had another good evening, laughing, talking, and getting to know each other. He was everything she ever wanted in a man—strong, kind, passionate, intelligent, fun, charming, and totally gorgeous. She loved the way she felt when she was with him. They ended the night with a tender, passionate kiss that left her smiling all the way home. And so their romance began.

"Ma'am?…ma'am?…Excuse me, ma'am?" Celeste was jolted back to reality by a gruff woman's voice.

"I'm sorry," she replied, realizing she hadn't been paying attention.

"Are you going to buy that filet?" the woman asked.

"No," Celeste replied. "It's all yours."

Celeste stepped aside and pushed her shopping cart out of the way. She realized that her head was now pounding, and she felt sick to her stomach. An overwhelming sense of sorrow and pain came over her. Connor was gone forever. The man who had once kissed her passionately and touched her soul had vanished from the face of the earth. She desperately wanted to hold him just one last time.

The thought that he had ceased to exist gripped her with a powerful sense of sadness, helplessness, and fear. Her feelings continued to build until she was overcome by them and could no longer escape. As hard as she tried, she was unable to fight back the emotions that flooded her mind and heart. Celeste bolted out of the grocery store, leaving her half-full shopping cart behind.

When she reached the car, she realized her hands were shaking, making it difficult to get the key out of her purse. She struggled for a moment, then was able to unlock the car and jump into the driver's seat. Celeste felt hurried, frantic. There was nowhere she had to be; yet she was certain there was something she was supposed to do. She just wished she could figure out what.

As Celeste started the car, the tears began to flow uncontrollably. She had no idea where to go but started driving anyway. She drove in circles for hours, the tears rushing down her cheeks like a rapidly flowing river. Her environment and her surroundings soon faded into the background, and the only thing she could see was the road in front of her. The path, it seemed, led nowhere. She knew where she was but felt so lost and alone. She didn't know where to go or what to do. Her pain was closing in on her, suffocating her. Celeste couldn't stay in this place. It hurt too much. She had to get out—and fast. She decidedly pointed her car in the direction of the office and sped to her escape.

When she walked through the doors of D & D's Accounting, her boss, Jeremy, looked up at her, startled. He was a scrawny little man with a pointed nose and round metal glasses.

"Celeste!" Jeremy said with a hint of delight. "I didn't expect to see you tonight."

She just stood frozen at the front door, paralyzed by the emotions that had brought her here in the first place.

"Are you okay? Are you sick?" Jeremy asked with concern. He had always had a soft spot for Celeste. Everyone in the office knew he was smitten with her. Everyone, that is, except Celeste. She was oblivious to his attraction. She just thought he was being nice. Little did she know that Jeremy had been thrilled when she and Dave separated. He secretly hoped they would get divorced so he could ask her out.

Celeste peered back at him through puffy, red eyes. Her pale, expressionless face resembled that of a ghostly white china doll, and her body felt limp and lifeless. She strained to reply.

"I'm…fine," she croaked weakly, slowly heading to the safety and security of her office.

She closed the door behind her and took a deep breath. *Free at last.* Then she sat at her desk, pulled out her calculator, and got to work. Soon the pain, the emotions, and the grief were replaced by hundreds of numbers, the droning hum of her computer, and the clinking sound of her calculator. She had now fully entered the physical world, a place where dreams and feelings could be left behind. Facts and figures now filled up her mind, and she was lulled into a place where she could feel nothing but the draft coming in the window behind her and the plastic buttons of the calculator beneath her fingertips.

She had successfully escaped that horrible place she had been trapped in. Everything was okay now. Celeste had used this technique many times before, throwing herself into her work to numb her pain or loneliness. With accounting, that was easy to do. It was a mundane, boring job requiring concentration and thinking, but no creativity or emotion.

Celeste had never really liked her job, but it was a good distraction, and it paid well. She remembered once aspiring to become an artist who painted glorious ocean scenes. She and Connor would sit at the beach, watching the soothing rhythm of the waves and the brilliant colors of the sunset. It was all so quiet and peaceful. Being at the beach soothed her soul and filled her with an uplifting stillness and a sense of completeness. It had helped that Connor was with her. The world always seemed crisper and sharper when was he was around. It was as if everything just came to life when they were together.

Her dreams of becoming an artist were short-lived. Her dad, who had always encouraged her creativity, had passed away of a heart attack just as she was about to enter college. Once he was gone, her mother—struggling to survive as a single parent—encouraged her to pursue a more practical career. "Art doesn't pay the bills," she would always caution. "Make sure you find a career that allows you to support yourself."

When she and Connor split, she lost her inspiration and opted to major in accounting. She threw herself into her studies and found them a very effective way to hide from her emotions and lessen the sense of loss she felt. Dave had met her at that point and assumed she was a driven, career-minded woman with an eye for business and a strong desire to excel in the corporate world. He believed they were so much alike. Or at least he wanted to. He never knew of her passion for art or love of nature. And she never really shared them with him. That part of her life, the essence of who she really was, had disappeared with Connor.

"What am I even doing here?" she asked herself. "I don't even like accounting, and yet this is the first place I come to when I'm upset. I don't even know who I am anymore. This isn't who I was supposed to be." Celeste packed up her belongings and shut down her computer. It was time to head home.

An empty, quiet, dark house awaited her. Her husband hadn't lived there in several months, and five-year-old Chip was staying with his grandma for a few days. Soon Celeste fell into a deep, dreamless sleep—which seemed fitting, considering the circumstances. All that awaited her in the morning was another long day at the office filled with numbers, and a mundane desk job. Her dreams, her passion, somehow had escaped her.

CHAPTER 2
SOMEDAY

*A*s Celeste drove home from work the next day, she began thinking about Connor again. She was exhausted from a long day at the office, and her mind was filled with dancing numbers and dollar signs. Her eyes stung from fatigue. Then his smiling face appeared in her head. It was a welcome sight!

She seemed to think of Connor a lot lately. Since his passing, she just couldn't get him out of her mind. There was so much she wanted to say to him. She felt like they had unfinished business. She had hoped to see him and talk to him again, but now that was impossible. How could she ever resolve her feelings and find the closure she so desperately needed?

Celeste began sobbing uncontrollably. She struggled to see the road ahead of her through tear-filled eyes. The landscape became a fuzzy blur of moonlight and shadowy trees. The world around her spun into an unrecognizable mix of darkness streaked with occasional rays of dim light. As she drove blindly ahead, she felt as if she were plunging into nothingness. And she didn't even care.

She would have continued in her oblivious state, but somehow, out of nowhere, she heard a very clear and distinct male voice pop into her head. She thought that surely she must have imagined it, because it sounded like Connor.

Pay attention.

Suddenly a deer darted out in front of her, its startled eyes aglow from the blazing gold headlights. Blood pulsed through her veins as she abruptly swerved her car to the right, narrowly missing the animal. With her heart still pounding, she took a deep breath and tried to regain her composure.

"That was close," she said aloud to herself. "Stay focused, Celeste. Keep it together."

Although she was alone in her car, she noticed a distinct presence. It felt like Connor was somehow with her. First the voice, and now this? Surely she must be losing her mind! Even so, she had an irresistible urge to talk to him. Maybe it was silly or useless, but she couldn't fight this desire brimming inside of her. She didn't just want communication with her deceased former love; she *needed* it—even if it was one-sided. She began to have a conversation as if he were right there with her.

"I'm so sorry," she sobbed. "I'm sorry I didn't stay in touch with you and try to be a part of your life in some way. I'm sorry I wasn't there for you or able to help you. I'm sorry for the night I left you. I'm sorry I didn't let you get closer to me or tell you that I love you. I'm just so sorry."

Tears streamed down Celeste's face like the rain on a shiny glass window, and she gasped for air. What she wanted most right now was to know that Connor still existed somehow, somewhere. She wanted proof that his spirit lived on. She wanted to know that he was alive and well in heaven. Although she had been raised Christian, her faith had faded as she'd grown older. Life's circumstances, unanswered prayers, and the cynical, materialistic world around her had left Celeste with doubts and questions. She now wondered if God and the afterlife even existed at all. She wanted to believe. She just didn't know how.

Right after she spoke to Connor, a song came on the radio. The words caught her attention, and she stopped crying long enough to listen. It was a tune by Nickelback titled "Someday."

For a brief moment, Celeste noticed a tingling sensation run down her spine. She felt like Connor was speaking directly to her through this song. It felt as if he were trying to respond to her. Were the words to this song meant for her? Did he somehow hear her cries? Was he trying to tell her he was going to help her in some way?

"No," thought Celeste. "You're being ridiculous. This is all just a coincidence. Connor can't hear you or help you—he's dead."

Somehow, even though her rational, logical mind told her this, her heart told her otherwise. Maybe Connor really was alive in the afterlife. Maybe he really could hear her. She needed to know the truth. She wanted answers. Celeste did the only thing she could think to do. She focused all of her love and energy on Connor. She gathered her strength and with a powerful, heartfelt plea, she spoke aloud to Connor once again.

"Oh, Connor!" she cried. "I just really want to know that you're okay."

She pulled into her driveway, parked her car, and stumbled in through the front door of her tan brick ranch. She was overcome with sorrow. It was very draining physically, mentally, and emotionally. Celeste felt totally depleted of all energy, very thankful that Chip was still staying at her mother's house. She was so exhausted that she just wanted to collapse right there on the floor. But she knew she needed to eat something first.

She grabbed a slice of pizza from the fridge, popped it into the microwave, and poured herself a glass of cabernet. She ate quickly, gulped down a few glasses of wine, and then snatched her fuzzy, blue pajamas from her top dresser drawer. She changed right away, brushed her teeth, and then fell into bed. It was only 8:00 p.m., but Celeste just couldn't stay awake any longer. Her exhaustion, combined with the effects of the wine, left her powerless. She fell into a sound sleep.

Next thing she knew, Celeste was in an unfamiliar office. The room was plain and bright, with grey, wall-to-wall carpeting and off-white cubicles. She was working side by side in one of the cubes with a woman she had never met. The lady had wavy, shoulder-length, reddish-orange hair and shiny, blue eyes. Celeste struggled to connect a battery to some sort of small metal device, but was having trouble. The woman kindly took the battery and helped Celeste to connect it. The lady then placed a variety of letter tiles onto the desk. Celeste began arranging them into clever words, kind of like in a Scrabble game. She was proud of her nifty creations, but her coworker didn't seem pleased. The woman shook her head no and rearranged the letters into her own word. When Celeste looked down to see what the lady had come up with, she was confused to see *T-E-I-S-H-A*.

"Teisha?" she thought. *What is that supposed to mean? Why did she get rid of my words and replace them with that?* She thought it must be a girl's name, but the woman's actions didn't make any sense to her.

The sound of the neighbor's dog barking awakened Celeste out of her dreamy slumber. She looked at the clock. It was 11:11 p.m. She remembered her strange dream and had an odd feeling that it meant something. It seemed like some sort of a lesson or message. Tomorrow she would try to unravel the clues. Celeste drifted back to sleep with images of Connor's face smiling at her. When she awoke again, it was 4:44 a.m.

This time Celeste headed to the kitchen and made herself a cup of hazelnut coffee. Sitting at the computer, she was determined to make sense of her unusual dream. She went to a dream interpretation website and typed in "battery."

It returned, "To dream of a battery signifies life's energy." *Hmm, that's interesting,* Celeste thought.

Next she went to Google and typed in "teisha name meaning." She clicked on the first entry and read:

Teisha *is a girl's name. It is a variant of Aisha*

and means "alive and well."

Alive and well! Celeste got the chills and was filled with an eerie feeling. Last night she had pleaded with Connor to let her know he was okay. Was this dream his way of telling her he was? Was Connor trying to communicate with her from beyond the grave?

Celeste knew she wouldn't rest until she found the answers to these questions. She was fully awake now. She would open her mind and heart to any possible signs or connections to Connor. She prayed to God to let Connor communicate with her.

She laid out a pair of jeans and a favorite sky-blue T-shirt for that day and jumped into the shower. The warm water felt soothing and refreshing. As its stream cascaded down her body, it slowly washed away her recurring feelings of fear and sorrow. She could feel her energy returning bit by bit. When her shower was over, she was refreshed and ready to take on the world again.

CHAPTER 3
BUSINESS AS USUAL

*D*ave stood at the fake-marble bathroom sink in the motel room he had been staying in for several months. He stared at his reflection, carefully studying his facial features as he shaved. Although he was no longer a young college guy, he was still a good-looking man. His serious, green eyes conveyed both intelligence and diligence. His hair was as black as the night sky and was carefully gelled back into place. He was of average height and very thin. He had a neat-and-tidy, professional businessman look that suited his ambitious nature and strong desire for achievement and financial gain.

Dave was definitely the kind of man many women wanted. He was financially secure and could provide a woman with a comfortable life and many luxuries. He was someone who would always take care of his spouse, although he was preoccupied, emotionally distant, and often spent long hours at the office where he worked as director of finance.

He knew that many ladies in the office found him desirable, and some had even propositioned him. But Dave only had eyes for one woman: his college sweetheart and wife, Celeste. He hated that they had been separated for many months. They had been to counseling, but their sessions always seemed to end in a big argument. He wanted to send their son Chip to a private school; she wanted to keep him in a public school in their neighborhood, with his friends. He valued his career and getting ahead in life; she thought he needed to find a position that let him spend more time with his family. She wanted to spend summers in a cozy cottage on the lake; he wanted to travel to Paris and London. Their disagreements were numerous, and their moments of intimacy and affection had become rare. Somehow they had drifted apart, and Dave felt like he was married to a stranger. He once believed they had a lot in common, but now it seemed there was very little they agreed on. He longed for the days when they would discuss their ambitions and dreams.

Dave would never forget the fire in Celeste's eyes and how she was once so determined to succeed. It was almost as if she had been on a mission. Little did Dave know that her mission was to forget someone she loved with all her heart. Celeste had no desire to be a wealthy, sought-after businesswoman. Her only motivation to bury herself in her work was to numb the pain she felt after calling it quits with her one-and-only true love.

Dave had mistaken her escapism for ambition. He

had witnessed her working so hard toward achievement in her career and had assumed that meant she was very much like him. Lately, however, he was beginning to realize just how different they really were.

Luckily he was attracted to more than just her strong drive and ambition. Celeste was also a beautiful, kind-hearted woman. She took good care of him, always making sure he had a hot-cooked meal, clean clothes, and plenty of time to pursue his favorite hobby, golf. She was also a good mother, a talented accountant, and a sensitive lover. She was everything any man could ever want in a woman. Dave believed they could still make their relationship work. After all, they cared about each other enough to get married, so there must still be something there. Why would she marry him if she didn't love him?

Dave remembered the time he first saw her studying alone, late at night in the University of Pennsylvania library. She had looked very serious and so determined—much like him. He had been thrilled to find a motivated, hardworking woman. When he finally did talk to her, he noticed an underlying sadness in her eyes and eventually learned that she had once been in an abusive relationship with some jerk named Andy and had recently broken up with another boyfriend named Connor. He could tell that she no longer had any feelings for Andy; however, he always wondered about Connor. He feared that Celeste was still in love with him. But he asked her out anyway, figuring he could make her forget all about him. He was confident and knew he was quite a catch, so it was just a matter of time before her ex-boyfriend would be a distant memory.

Unfortunately, he was wrong. Celeste and Connor kept in touch for a few months after their breakup, sometimes meeting for lunch and sharing long, late-night phone conversations. There had been plenty of times when Dave tried to call Celeste in her dorm room, only to hear a busy signal. When he later asked who she was talking to for so long, her answer was always "Connor."

Celeste didn't know it, but Dave secretly kept tabs on her and even eavesdropped on her phone conversations several times. He would stand outside her dorm room and just listen. The walls were thin enough that he could hear most of what she said to Connor. And she almost always sounded so happy. She seemed to rely on him for advice about school, her career, and her relationships. She often joked with him, and they seemed to share many laughs. Sometimes the conversation would turn serious, and they would discuss their problems and their fears. One night Dave overheard Celeste crying. He stood outside her door, about to knock, when he heard her muffled sobs and realized she was talking to Connor. "You're the only one who ever really understood me," she cried.

Dave listened even more intently that night. He needed to know what was upsetting Celeste. She never said she loved Connor or that she wanted him back, but the tone in her voice was enough to convince him of the truth. On the phone, she talked about how they first met, the good times they shared, how he had saved her from that abusive jerk, Andy, and how he had become her most trusted "friend." It was clear to Dave that Connor was and always would be more than just a friend to Celeste. He remembered thinking that this man could be a real threat to his budding relationship with her. He was jealous of their meetings, and the way she smiled when she talked about him. And hearing her words to Connor that night only added to his jealousy. Were they discussing their future? Would Celeste and Connor be getting back together? Where did that leave him?

Dave was so relieved when he learned the source of Celeste's tears. Connor and Celeste weren't talking about their relationship; they were saying good-bye. Connor had accepted a teaching job in Italy! Dave recalled his immense joy and relief when he learned that his girlfriend's former beau was moving so far away. He would now have Celeste all to himself. Those two certainly couldn't carry on any sort of a relationship when they were thousands of miles apart! This was definitely good news for Dave. Celeste was all his now.

And for a while, she was. Celeste graduated from college, threw herself into her career, and eventually agreed to marry him. At first she refused his proposal, explaining that she needed to establish her career. Then she wanted to save more money. After she had achieved both of these goals, she was still reluctant because of the high divorce rate and wanted to make sure her marriage would last forever. There were times when Dave wondered exactly what she was really waiting for. What was she afraid of? He never found out, but he was able to convince her that he would be a good husband. One day, she told him she was finally ready to get married.

She was a devoted wife, eager to please him, and ready to start a family. She really seemed to value her marriage and her new role. She did whatever she could to make sure he was happy and well taken care of. She supported his career and was agreeable to all of his ideas for their future. They really seemed to be on the same page. Dave was thrilled that he had married the perfect woman.

But despite her outward appearance and actions, there was still always an underlying sadness about her. He knew she missed Connor deeply, and though he tried, Dave could never seem to fill the void that Connor's absence had left. One day he realized the truth: she was clearly still in love with him. That didn't discourage Dave, though. Being the confident, ambitious, goal-oriented man he was, he was still certain that one day, all of that would change. Once they had children, Celeste would no doubt be so wrapped up in her new life as a mother that she would fully embrace it and forget about Connor. What was missing in her life was a baby, not a particular man. He was determined to give her a child as soon as possible and didn't waste any time getting her pregnant.

His plan seemed to work, because after Charles David—affectionately called Chip—was born, Celeste's mood noticeably brightened. She seemed glowing and happy and was thrilled with her new role as a mother. She smiled often and was even more affectionate with Dave. Her sadness had finally seemed to fade into the background.

However, it didn't last. A few years after Chip was born, the disagreements and arguments began. Celeste didn't seem to have the same priorities as Dave. She was no longer the ambitious career woman who was so driven to succeed. Instead, she valued quiet time and would often sit outside by herself on the porch after Chip had gone to sleep. Dave wondered how she could have changed so much. They had seemed so alike when they first met in college. Was it possible that he never knew the real Celeste? Was the therapist right?

In couples therapy, the counselor had said that Dave had never taken the time to really get to know his wife, which was the source of part of their conflict. She also said that Celeste was still holding on to feelings from the past, and until she let go of them, they would continue to interfere with the relationship.

Then one day their counselor had suggested that they separate to try to work out their issues. Dave was against the idea, fearing his wife would run off to Italy to be with Connor. Celeste wholeheartedly embraced the suggestion and believed that time apart might bring them closer together. He had hoped she was right. Tonight he would find out.

He would be meeting with Celeste privately this evening to discuss the fate of their relationship. He clearly knew what he wanted. He wanted her. Not just her presence, but all of her: mind, body, heart, and soul. He longed to move back into their home. He wanted his wife back. Dave hoped it wasn't too late for them. He had to look his best and do whatever he could to sweep her off her feet.

He splashed on Celeste's favorite aftershave and gave himself one last check in the mirror. "Looking good," he said to himself. "How could she turn this down?"

Dave switched off the bathroom light and went into the hotel bedroom. It was decorated in rich shades of green and burgundy. The carpet was a thick, plush, forest green, and the queen-size bed was covered in a flowered bedspread. The room was small but clean and comfortable. Dave had spent so many nights alone here and was more than ready to return to his wife. He walked over to the mahogany desk next to the bed and carefully removed a neatly typed sheet of paper from the drawer. He thoroughly studied his notes once again, so he would be prepared for this very important meeting. This time, his notes were not a financial plan or a corporate strategy; they were his plan to win Celeste back. Dave approached his relationship much like he would a business meeting. He was organized. He was meticulous. He was persuasive. He just hoped his plan would work.

He carefully rehearsed his "presentation" to Celeste. First he would enter with a smile, present her with flowers and a diamond bracelet, and shower her with compliments. A little romance would surely kick things off. He imagined the scene that would follow. He would ignite the passion with a kiss that would leave her wanting more, begging him to continue. He wouldn't talk about their problems or the growing distance between them. In fact, Dave strategized that it was best not to say much at all. He would just continue the passion and the kissing until she gave in to her desire. He would be able to tell when that was by her body language and the way her body felt against his. If her muscles felt limp and relaxed, then she was ready for more.

After that, he would carry her to the bedroom, where the passion would escalate. Then when he finally spoke, he would compliment her again and tell her about his promotion. Celeste surely wouldn't be able to turn down a good-looking, romantic, passionate, successful man. Finally, he would tell her he was moving back in, and she would gladly welcome him with open arms! Dave was certain his plan would work. Just like in the business world, he was calm, confident, and driven. But was his detailed strategy enough to permanently win back the heart of the woman he loved?

CHAPTER 4
HEART AND SOUL

Celeste was so glad it was Saturday. She really needed a day off. She missed little Chip and wanted to spend some quality time with him. She went to pick him up at her mother's red brick bungalow, the home she had grown up in. She knocked, and her mother answered the door right away.

Mrs. Moore was a short, heavy-set, kindly woman in her late fifties. She had the same golden hair as Celeste, only it was short, curly, and streaked with shades of silver. She wore mauve lipstick and round, gold glasses that perfectly framed her sky-blue eyes.

"Hello, honey," she said as she hugged her daughter. "Chip is all ready to go. He is excited to visit the park with you."

"Thanks, Mom." Celeste smiled warmly. "It should be a nice day."

"Mommmmmy!" Chip chirped excitedly. He ran to Celeste, his wavy, sand-colored hair bouncing. He looked up at her with enthusiastic, blue eyes and happily jumped into her arms, covering her face with soft, wet kisses.

"I missed you too, sweetie," she said as she softly kissed his tiny cheek. "Are you ready to go to the park?"

"You bet!" he exclaimed.

They loaded the car and were soon on their way to Perry Park. As they drove to their destination, a warm autumn sun flickered through the trees onto their faces. The air was filled with the smell of damp leaves and campfire. Celeste noticed today how rich and vibrant the fall colors were. She admired the shades of rust, amber, and crimson. Somehow this morning she felt more hopeful and peaceful. The world around her seemed lit up like a stage, and she was ready to see what the day ahead would bring.

As they arrived at the park, Chip chattered happily about all that he was going to do while they were there. He loved the swings and couldn't wait to glide through the air. He jumped out of the car and darted to the swings. "Wait for Mommy, please, Chip!" Celeste called protectively. But he was already way ahead of her.

Celeste jogged to catch up. She found a nice park bench near the playground and sat down to watch her son. His smile was contagious, and she found herself grinning as she watched him sing and swing. He was a remarkable little boy, and she was so thankful to have him in her life.

Chip had always been so easygoing and wise beyond his years. He instinctively seemed to know how to comfort and console others. He was often found making a special card for a sick relative, offering a tissue to a crying child, or giving his advice on complicated matters. Although he was just five years old, sometimes he felt like an adult to Celeste. His insight into human emotions and the way the world worked was just amazing. She had no idea how he could know the things he did.

Celeste was also grateful for her son's cheery disposition and ability to always see the bright side of every situation. He was an eternal optimist. If something didn't go his way, he wouldn't cry or sulk like most kids. Chip would instead tell his mom, "Sometimes when stuff doesn't work out, it's not meant to be. Sometimes we need to learn things. We can't always have our way."

What young child says that? For many, the world revolves only around them, and they expect to get everything their little hearts desire. When they don't, they cry, stomp their feet, and become very frustrated. But not Chip. He took everything in stride. He was truly an amazing child who brightened her days and actually taught her a thing or two about love and life.

She only wished that she and his daddy could work out their differences. Celeste was meeting with her estranged husband tonight to discuss their future. She hoped he would move back into the house with her and Chip. Dave was a good man, but they disagreed on important issues, such as financial matters and how to raise and educate Chip. Celeste did love Dave, and she had great respect and admiration for him. But they were so different, and there was little passion left between them these days. For one, Dave was a workaholic, a person who valued money and career above all else. He believed the best way to be a good husband and father was to be a good provider.

Celeste, on the other hand, valued love and relationships above all else. She obviously wanted enough money to survive, but material possessions and wealth were at the bottom of her list. She appreciated the simple things in life: a warm embrace, a gentle smile, a glorious sunset, or a day sitting at the beach watching the waves. She loved nature and felt more peaceful and connected whenever she was outdoors. Celeste didn't like to be cooped up inside the house or stuck at the office. She would much rather spend her days at the park, like today.

Celeste also was a kind, caring person who made friends easily. She was a good listener and was always ready to lend a hand to someone in need. She was invited to many social events, although she turned a lot of them down because she didn't want to take too much time away from her son. She did regularly accept lunch invitations from coworkers and had many friends, both male and female.

Unfortunately, Dave was a bit possessive and jealous, so he was uncomfortable with Celeste having male friends. He had accused her of cheating on him when she had come home late from work a few times. Celeste found his concerns silly and unnecessary. She had always remained faithful to her husband and didn't appreciate his lack of trust. Sometimes she wished he was more...like Connor.

Again she thought about her deceased ex-boyfriend.

Celeste was still shocked and sad. *He was on his way home, and he wanted to see me! We were so close to reconnecting again.* She wondered if Connor had still had feelings for her before he died. Could that be why he wanted to see her again after all these years? Or was she just engaging in wishful thinking?

Maybe he didn't have *romantic* feelings for her. Perhaps he just wanted to hang out with an old friend. Now she would never know the truth! She wished she could just talk to him and get some answers.

Then Celeste remembered her unusual experiences with the song and the dream. She decided to try something different. She would ask Connor for a sign. Celeste had doubts it would work, but it was certainly worth a try. She had nothing to lose. "Connor, if you still had feelings for me, please send me a sign," she whispered.

She looked around the park, hoping to see something that would answer her question. She noticed several chickadees fluttering by and chirping. She gazed at the rich, vibrant colors of the leaves on the tress. She saw children running and playing, and parents watching. She saw dogs playing catch. But she noticed nothing that would qualify as a sign. Finally she gave up.

Celeste began to wonder again if everything she had experienced was just coincidence or wishful thinking. Maybe Connor was just plain dead. Maybe there really wasn't an afterlife. And even if there was, that didn't mean he could hear her and communicate with her. Celeste feared she was just being ridiculous and letting her grief and sadness cloud her judgment. Did she seriously think she could communicate with the dead?

Even if Connor could hear her, that didn't necessarily mean he would be willing or able to reach out to her. Maybe he had never really cared about her that much after all. Besides, if he did love her and had never stopped, then why didn't they stay together? As these thoughts ran through her mind, Celeste's good mood faded, and she began to sink into a deep depression. Her whole body felt sluggish and heavy. She could hardly move.

"Mommmm!" yelled Chip from his swing.

Celeste turned in his direction and asked what he needed.

"Can you push me?"

"Sure, honey," Celeste replied, although she secretly wished he hadn't asked. Her energy was totally depleted, and pushing Chip was like trying to knock over a brick wall. Her arms were weak. She could hardly move, let alone push a forty-pound child. She didn't want to disappoint him, so she forced herself to continue. She would do anything for her precious son. She would even move mountains if she had to.

After several minutes Celeste told Chip it was time to go. They got into the car and headed for home. The ride was uncomfortably silent.

"Mommy, what's wrong?" asked little Chip, sensing her sorrow.

"Mommy's just sad," Celeste replied.

"Why are you sad?"

"Mommy's friend Connor died," she said. "He was important to me, and I miss him very much."

"But it's okay, Mommy," Chip said reassuringly. "When people die, they go to heaven. They get to be angels. And angels can help people. He will help you, Mommy. He will be your angel."

Celeste smiled at her sweet son in the rearview mirror. His precious, innocent face was filled with so much love and hope. His ocean-blue eyes overflowed with compassion. His thick, sandy hair was tousled about from running and playing in the park. She adored the little guy!

There he goes again, thought Celeste. *Acting wise and trying to console me.* And his words actually did give her some comfort and a spark of hope. She wanted Connor to be alive and well in the afterlife. She wanted him to help her and be her angel. She just didn't know if that was even possible. But if it was, would Connor even want to help her? He had left a message on her cell phone before he died, but they hadn't actually spoken in years.

"It's too quiet in here," she said. "Let's turn on the radio." As Celeste scanned the channels, she heard a familiar tune. It was the song "Someday." *There's that song again!* Celeste found it odd that she had heard it twice since yesterday. She hadn't heard it in months before that. Once again, she figured it must just be a coincidence. That was the only reasonable explanation.

After that song, another familiar tune came on. It was "Wish You Were Here" by Pink Floyd. She hadn't heard it in ages! She remembered how much Connor had loved Pink Floyd. This was the song that most reminded her of him. She pictured Connor's beautiful face and smile. *I do wish you were here, Connor*, she thought.

"Mom, I like this song," said Chip suddenly from the backseat.

"You do?" asked Celeste with surprise.

"Yeah, it's cool."

The two of them listened to the comforting guitar music and enjoyed the moment. Celeste felt a tiny bit better and a little less alone. When the song ended, she decided to change the station and heard "Hey You." She felt a buzz of electricity run through her.

"Another Pink Floyd song!" she said aloud. "That's pretty strange."

"Pink Floyd must be really popular, Mom!" Chip exclaimed.

"Well, they were, many years ago," said Celeste.

I love Pink Floyd! Are you sure you don't like Pink Floyd? She could still hear Connor's words from the night they first met. The songs somehow brought her an odd sense of peace and comfort.

As she drove quietly home, taking in the fall scenery around her, Celeste noticed a hawk circling overhead. The bird swooped lower and lower until it was directly over her car. She watched it coast through the air, moving swiftly and deliberately as it scoped out the area. She thought of how strong and confident the bird looked. The hawk behaved like he knew exactly who he was and understood his purpose. He appeared to be on some sort of mission. Celeste wished she knew what her purpose in life was. Some days she just wandered aimlessly, trying to figure out what she was supposed to be doing and what she wanted to accomplish. She might be an accountant, but her career had never really felt right to her. It was just something she did to earn a living. On the outside she appeared to be doing quite well. But on the inside, she was totally lost. She had never seemed to quite find her place in the world.

She thought back to a dream she'd had a few days ago. The same reddish-haired lady from the office dream with the letter tiles had appeared again. Like the hawk circling above, she had also seemed to be on some sort of mission. She had stared intently at Celeste, her blue eyes aglow with tiny flecks of violet and indigo. She had come to deliver an important message.

"Remember...your life's purpose is just what you choose to do," she began. "But your *soul's purpose* is for eternity." Then the woman disappeared.

Celeste was still puzzled by this message. She thought she understood the first part: Her life's purpose was being an accountant and a mom. That's what she had chosen to do with her time on earth. But what about this "soul purpose" the lady had referred to? What did that mean? How was she supposed to figure that out?

A commercial came on the car radio. Celeste changed the station. Immediately she heard a third Pink Floyd song: "Learning to Fly." A cool, tingly sensation ran through her body, and she thought of Connor again. She knew in her soul that something interesting and unusual was going on. She could feel it. Celeste listened intently to the lyrics as she pulled up to a red light, still gazing at the hawk soaring above her.

She wondered if Connor was learning to fly, wherever he was. Maybe he was adjusting to his new environment. Was it possible he was trying to share his new life with her? Was he trying to talk to her somehow? Celeste still didn't know what to make of all of this. *Get a grip, Celeste*, she thought. *Stop reading too much into things*.

Her rational, analytical mind took over. She was probably just causing these songs to appear because she was thinking of him. That must be it! Or maybe it was because Connor had been on her mind. *When we're thinking of someone or something, we naturally notice stuff that reminds us of them.* This wasn't communication from Connor's spirit; it was simply her being more sensitive and observant of songs that reminded her of him. Sometimes it was so hard to separate fact from fiction—especially when emotions were involved. Still, a part of her hoped all of this was something more.

I don't know if you can hear me, Connor, she thought, *but it sure would be nice if you could.* Just as the traffic light turned green, Celeste's eyes fixed on the license plate of the car in front of her. Her heart skipped a beat. I HEAR U, the plate read.

Holy shit! This is getting weirder by the minute, she thought. So many questions flooded her racing mind. This was just too unreal to comprehend. Maybe she was dreaming and would wake up soon. Maybe she had lost touch with reality. Or just maybe…Connor really was trying to talk to her.

Once home, Celeste helped Chip get out of the car and they headed inside. Still in a fog, she hung his red baseball jacket in the closet and began unzipping her grey fleece sweatshirt when something on her left sleeve near her shoulder caught her eye. She looked more closely and discovered a chunk of mud—in the form of a perfect heart!

She felt an electric bolt shoot through her. She couldn't believe what she was seeing. Where had this come from? How did it end up on her sleeve? And, more important, how did it become a perfect heart? Celeste had never seen a chunk of mud that looked like a heart before, let alone one on her arm. Was this the sign she had asked for? First the songs, then the license plate, and now this. She couldn't have caused any of this; it wouldn't make any sense.

Celeste honestly didn't know what was going on with her, but something bizarre was definitely happening. Her recent experiences were almost magical. But she lived in the real world, where everything must be proven concretely. As an accountant, she was used to dealing with numbers and facts. She couldn't just accept weird happenings as communications from the dead. How was that even possible? She needed more proof, but she had no idea how she was going to get it. How could she prove something she couldn't see or touch?

CHAPTER 5
RECONCILIATION

*C*eleste nervously combed her golden hair and put on another coat of mascara. She knew that Dave would be there any minute, and somehow she felt like she must look and act perfect to win him back. Despite their differences, she still wanted him in her life. He took good care of her and Chip and was emotionally stable. She could really use some support right now! She had felt lost, confused, and emotional lately. Connor's death and the events that followed had left her in a fog. She feared she was losing touch with reality. She needed answers and explanations.

Celeste needed life to make sense again. Dave would be able to help her. He was so level-headed and grounded. He always had a well-thought-out strategy for addressing every issue. He would be able to find a reasonable explanation for the strange occurrences in her life. He would know what to do. She was thankful her young son Chip was sleeping soundly because she really needed some private discussion time with her husband.

The doorbell rang, and Celeste nervously darted to the front door to answer it. "Hello, Celeste!" Dave greeted her with a huge smile. His jet-black hair was slicked back neatly in place, and he was wearing black dress pants, a crisp white shirt, and a blue tie. His green eyes looked affectionately at her. "You look gorgeous! I've missed you, darling," he said as he handed her a bouquet of daisies.

"Thank you! I've missed you too." She smiled warmly.

"And there's more," he said excitedly as he placed a glittering diamond bracelet around her wrist.

"It's beautiful," she gasped. "But it really wasn't necessary. You shouldn't spend so much money on me."

"You deserve it," he replied. "I want you to have the very best of everything."

The best of everything. To Celeste, that meant something far different than Dave could ever fathom. Diamond bracelets meant nothing compared to the great rewards of love, peace, fulfillment, and joy—things that money just couldn't buy. At least Dave was trying, though. He wanted her to be happy. He was making an effort to please her. She had to give him credit for that.

Dave stepped into the house they had shared for five years. He took her into his arms and kissed her passionately. A thrill of excitement and lust ran through her body. But Dave was always so serious and busy with work. He hadn't kissed her like that in years. Where was this coming from?

The kissing continued. His mouth met hers wildly, and the desire between them quickly escalated. Celeste's body softened, and she felt like putty in his arms. He began removing her tan silk blouse. Before long, there was a pile of clothes lying right on the welcome mat at the front door. They hadn't even moved from the spot!

Celeste felt her heart pounding. She forgot all about their problems and ached to make love to him. And he wanted her more than he had ever wanted anything—or anyone—in his life. He was determined to win back his wife. Dave scooped Celeste up and carried her to their bedroom. She surrendered to him. They made love for hours, not speaking a word but getting lost in each other.

When they finally came up for air, Celeste was drenched in sweat and thoroughly exhausted. But she felt a sense of relief and contentment. Maybe there was hope for them, after all. She wished that Dave would move back into their house with her and Chip. She desperately needed emotional support right now.

After what seemed like an eternity, they finally spoke. "Wow, Celeste. That was incredible!" Dave exclaimed. "You look and feel fantastic. You must be taking good care of yourself lately."

"I try," Celeste mumbled, barely able to get the words out. She still felt breathless.

"So, what have you been up to?" he asked, genuinely interested. "Tell me about your job and your life."

"I've been busy working and taking care of Chip, as usual. Nothing out of the ordinary," Celeste lied, wondering if it was the right time to tell Dave about the bizarre coincidences involving Connor. "What about you?"

"Well, you know me. I've been swamped at work. Long days. Most days, I work about twelve hours. But it's all paying off."

"Oh?"

"I just got a promotion, Celeste," he said. "They made me vice president of finance. You, me, and Chip can live the good life. We can move into a bigger, nicer house and send him to the best private school in town."

"That's great, honey. Congratulations!" she said sincerely, although a nagging fear in her heart kept her from being excited about his other ideas. She had no desire to send Chip to an expensive private school, and she certainly didn't want to move into a big fancy house. She liked a quiet, simple life, not one filled with lavish gifts, luxuries, and snooty private schools. Although she objected strongly, she kept quiet for now, because she didn't want to upset Dave or ruin his moment. And she feared he wouldn't stay with her if she protested. They had already been on rocky ground. She didn't want to disturb the peace, especially since everything was going so well so far tonight.

"I have more good news," Dave began. "I brought my things. I'm moving back into the house tonight. Isn't that great?"

Dave was returning to her. This is what she had been hoping for. Oddly, she didn't feel happy. She was relieved, of course; she didn't like living without a man in her life. Still, there was this nagging feeling that something wasn't right. This didn't *feel* right. They hadn't really resolved anything yet, or come to any agreements or understandings. The same issues that had driven them apart were still there. Her husband just didn't seem to understand her. How were they going to find common ground? Nonetheless, he was her husband. It's not like she had better options. Besides, Chip had missed him terribly and needed his daddy around. Celeste managed a smile and gave Dave a warm hug.

"That's wonderful! Chip will be so excited to see you tomorrow morning," Celeste said, straining to display some excitement. "He's sound asleep, and I don't want to wake him. He probably wouldn't be able to get back to sleep after seeing you."

"That's okay, babe. I'm tired, too. I can wait until morning. Right now, I just want to sleep with my beautiful wife. I'm such a lucky guy to have you."

They wrapped their arms around each other and fell into a peaceful slumber. For the first time in many months, Celeste felt safe and protected. Her husband was there for her to lean on. In the morning, she would tell him all about Connor and the strange happenings in her life. He would help her sort everything out.

Celeste awoke at 4:44 a.m. again. *That's odd. What's up with the repeating numbers?* she thought. Despite her growing curiosity, she was way too tired to think about it now. This would have to wait. She rolled over and snuggled up behind Dave to go back to sleep. As she put her arms around him and pressed her body against his, she suddenly noticed someone or something press against her back. She paused to observe. Was this just her imagination? Was she actually still sleeping and just thought she was awake? No, she was alert and completely awake, and the sensation was still there. She could clearly feel a body behind her, putting pressure on the back side of her, just like she was doing to Dave.

Had Chip snuck into their room without her noticing? No, this body was too big to be Chip. It felt like it had the size and strength of a full-grown man. Her heart raced, and fear pulsed through her veins. She wanted to scream or jump right out of bed, but she was paralyzed. *Who the hell is that?* she thought, too afraid to move or look. *Did someone break into our house?*

Her mind flashed back to her abusive ex, Andy, and the horrible things he had done to her. Her panic heightened. She recalled the feeling of being totally powerless against him. Was Andy here in her bed to hurt her again? Should she wake Dave or keep quiet? Maybe if she lay still enough, he would go away.

Celeste's instincts told her not to wake Dave. She had no idea why, since Dave might actually be able to fight this man off of her. Somehow, she believed it was best to keep quiet. Oddly, she sensed this was a private matter between her and the unknown man who was touching her. So she lay there silently for several minutes as she assessed the situation. She could still feel him. His warmth covered her back like a thick blanket, and his body firmly pressed against hers with strength and stillness. He didn't utter a sound or make a move. He just lay there, snuggled behind her.

As Celeste continued to observe the energy of this unknown person, she began to feel calmer. She noticed that the sensation of him felt comforting and strangely familiar. She felt as if this man, whoever he was, actually cared about her. But the fact remained: she had not invited him into her home, let alone her bed. He was an uninvited guest, an intruder. She tried to be as still and quiet as possible. Whoever he was, she wanted him to go away. "Please stop. Leave me alone," she pleaded silently. And then in an instant, he was gone.

Celeste sighed a breath of relief and calmed down, but she still felt a bit unsettled. She had never heard anyone come in or out of her room. Was this man really an intruder? She had never felt this person get up and leave, either. It was as if he had just vanished into thin air. With all the unusual happenings in her life, she feared she had accidentally invited an unwanted ghost into her home. Had this entity come to harm her? But he hadn't done anything to hurt her. In fact, he had actually seemed loving and affectionate. All he did was nestle behind her like she had snuggled behind Dave. He had seemed more interested in being with her than doing anything harmful or destructive.

Just then a thought occurred to her: A man who just wanted to be with her. A man who would never cause her harm and was always protective of her. Was it Connor? Had his spirit somehow visited her and actually lain down next to her in bed?

Although she longed to be with Connor again, the thought of his spirit touching her and floating around her house made her shudder. It just seemed so creepy. Celeste could handle the signs, the songs, and the strange coincidences. But she couldn't handle this. It had gone too far. She had crossed into uncharted territory now. She had entered an unknown world where the impossible suddenly seemed plausible. And it scared the living daylights out of her.

"Connor," she whispered. "If you're trying to tell me something, I'm listening. But please don't touch me like that again. And please—whatever you do—don't appear as a ghostly apparition, because that would really freak me out."

She noticed stirring in the bed next to her. Dave was awake. Had he heard her? "Who are you talking to, Celeste?" he mumbled sleepily.

"No one," Celeste lied. "I must have been talking in my sleep."

Dave bolted straight up in bed and angrily grabbed her shoulders. "Don't lie to me, Celeste! I heard you say his name and something about touching you!" he fumed jealously. "Is Connor in town? Are you sleeping with him?"

"No. Hell no. Why would you think that?"

"Then why are you talking to him?" Dave demanded.

"Okay, you're right. I do have something to tell you, but it's not what you think...Connor died," she said as a lump formed in her throat. She could feel the tears pooling in her eyes. Just saying the words made the sadness and longing for him return once again.

"What? Really? Man... That... It...sucks. Too bad for him," Dave stuttered. "But I must say, I'm kind of relieved. I was always afraid you would leave me for him. When we separated, that was my worst fear."

"Why would you think I would leave you for Connor? We hadn't spoken in years. Besides, I'm married to you. You're my husband, and I love you." As she uttered the words, she realized she felt more like she was talking to her brother than her husband. She was fond of Dave. She respected Dave. She loved Dave, but was she *in* love with him? That, she wasn't sure of. She had never been sure of that. Luckily, he didn't notice her lack of passion.

"I love you too, Celeste," he said sweetly. "Sorry I got so riled up. I just don't want to lose you. So then why were you talking to him?"

"Well, that's actually a complicated story. Why don't we start making breakfast, and I'll fill you in."

"Sounds great. I'm starving. I think I burned a thousand calories last night with you."

Celeste blushed and laughed. "Welcome back, Dave." She smiled.

***

The delicious smell of bacon and eggs filled their sunny kitchen. The yellow walls seemed even brighter and more inviting than usual. It was a gorgeous fall morning, and Celeste felt happy. She hoped that Dave would understand her experiences and help her work through them. It was so nice to have a man back in her life.

"So, tell me about this Connor thing. What happened? How did he die?"

Celeste explained about the plane crash and how Connor had been on his way home for good from Rome. She told him all about the strange experiences with the songs, the dream, and the heart-shaped chunk of mud. He sat listening, quietly and seriously. She left out the part about the person in their bed last night. When she finished, he was still silent. "What do you think?" Celeste inquired.

"I think you're still in love with him," Dave said coolly. "And to be honest, that disturbs me."

"What difference does it make how I feel about Connor?" Celeste asked, her irritation building. "He's dead, and our relationship was over a long time ago."

"Well, that's the point, Celeste. Your relationship was over a long time ago, but you still want to know how he felt about you?" Dave said, raising his voice. "For Christ's sake, you're speaking to a dead guy, asking him to send you signs to show he cares! And I'm supposed to be okay with that?"

"I'm sorry, Dave. I really don't want to hurt or upset you," Celeste said calmly. "I'm just trying to figure this all out. Do you believe Connor's spirit is actually around me? Is that why this bothers you so much? Do you somehow feel threatened by his presence in my life?"

Dave's anger quickly faded, and his face took on a much lighter expression. He was amused. He laughed a hearty, mocking laugh that filled the once-sunny room with doubt and ridicule.

"Oh, poor Celeste," he said. "I don't even know you anymore. You really are delusional. Can't you see, your obsession with this guy has you imagining things? Dead people can't communicate with us. They're dead."

Celeste felt the warm rush of blood to her face. Dave's words hurt and angered her. He could be so kind sometimes, but other times, he was downright cynical and mean.

"Is that what you think this is?" she fumed. "My *imagination*? I didn't expect any of this, and I certainly didn't create it—it just happened! It's not like I was sitting around with a Ouija board trying to conjure up his spirit or anything! What happened really surprised me—

and there's more, too!"

As Celeste howled her last words at Dave, she noticed little Chip standing by the table staring at them. His tiny face was wrinkled with troubled concern. "Mommy, Daddy, why are you yelling at each other?" he asked. "Are you getting a divorce?"

"Sorry, sweetie. Daddy and I just disagree about something," Celeste tried to explain comfortingly.

"Don't worry, guys," Chip said with a reassuring tone. "Everything is okay. I saw an angel last night!" Celeste froze. Dave shot her a penetrating, icy stare.

"Oh, great. You've dragged him into your psychosis!" Dave shouted.

"Mommy didn't do anything," Chip chimed in.

"Just tell us what happened," Celeste said calmly. "It was probably just a dream."

"No, Mom. It wasn't a dream," Chip protested. "I was sleeping. Then I felt someone touch my face. I thought it was you, so I woke up."

"Maybe it was a bug or your covers," Dave offered.

"No, Dad. It wasn't. I saw him."

"You saw who, Chip?"

"The angel. He was standing next to my bed smiling at me. He was all glowy white like angels are. But he didn't have wings. Or a halo. He looked...like a person, a man."

Celeste hesitated. "What did he look like, sweetie?" she asked.

"He had wavy brown hair and brown eyes. He was very nice. He said he was trying to visit Mommy, but she was too afraid and kept ignoring him and wanting him to go away. Oh, and he said I have good taste in music because I like Pink Floyd. Just like him!"

Oh, my gosh, Celeste thought. *Connor!*

"It really was just a dream," Dave explained. "You probably thought you woke up but actually didn't. That can happen sometimes. Let's just forget about it, okay?"

"Okay, Dad." Chip sounded disappointed. "But I wish it really was an angel. Mommy needs one. She's been very sad. I want Mommy to be happy."

"Don't worry, Chip. Mommy will be fine," Dave said soothingly. "I'm back to take care of her. We'll get her the help she needs."

Take care of her! The help she needs! Celeste found herself enraged by his comments. Who did he think he was, her savior? Did he think he could just send her off to some therapist to make all of this go away?

Celeste was now more certain than ever that she was not crazy. She and Chip had both felt someone touch them last night, and Chip had clearly seen Connor. He had described him perfectly, and he had never even met him or seen his picture! And Pink Floyd...that wasn't a dream. Connor was here; Celeste was sure of it. She had sent him away, so he had visited her son instead. What Celeste didn't fully understand was *why*.

CHAPTER 6
AN ANGEL TO WATCH OVER ME

A few weeks had passed since Dave had moved back in. Chip was so excited to have Daddy back, even though he only saw him sometimes. But nothing really changed. Dave was still working long hours, as usual, and still showering his family with gifts to express his love. Chip enjoyed the surprises—especially the new baseball cap, toy truck, and bike—but what he really needed most was his father's guidance and companionship. He also needed to feel secure, which was hard to do when he didn't know if Daddy would be leaving again or not. Chip really hoped his father would stay this time.

Outside his bedroom window, Chip could see only darkness, a full moon, and the porch lights of their neighbors. He was feeling very sleepy and knew that Mommy would be coming back soon to tuck him in.

Chip quietly knelt down beside his twin bed to say his prayers. His room was decorated in shades of green, his favorite color, and sported an airplane motif. He had always been fascinated by things in the sky and was often found looking up at the clouds, watching for birds, planes, helicopters, and hot-air balloons.

He never told Mommy, but he was also now on the lookout for his new friend. The angel had been visiting Chip regularly and said that his name was Connor. Chip never saw him come down from heaven; he always just appeared in Chip's room after the lights were out and his parents were sleeping. Chip was determined to catch the angel during his descent. Maybe tonight would be the night! "Dear God, please watch over Mommy and Daddy. Keep our family safe. Please help Mommy to be happy again. She still seems sad. And help Daddy to stop working so much. And please, please, please let my angel visit me tonight. I like him. Thank you. Amen."

Celeste walked into her son's room just as he ended his prayer. She loved that he had a good relationship with God and prayed regularly. She had lost that part of herself for a while and was glad her son had such a strong faith. "Ready for bed, sweetie?" she asked, gently stroking his soft, sandy hair.

"Yup. Is Daddy home?"

"No, sorry, hon. Daddy is still at work."

"He's always at work."

"I know, Chip," Celeste said sympathetically. "Daddy works hard. He wants us to have a good life."

"But doesn't he know that we already have a good life?" Chip asked.

"I guess he just wants better."

"What do you want, Mommy?"

"I want a kiss from my sweet boy," she said as she began to tickle him.

He laughed his cute little giggle and smothered her with little, wet kisses. "Good night, Mommy."

"Good night, sweetie," she replied as she switched off his hot-air balloon lamp.

Chip lay there very still and quiet for a while. He was determined to stay up and watch for the angel. When he was sure his mom was sleeping, he called out to him. "Pssst. Connor. Can you hear me?"

There was just silence. Where was he? When would he be coming to visit again?

"Hello?" Chip called.

But still no one answered. Chip was disappointed. He really wanted to see Connor tonight. What was keeping him? Weren't angels supposed to come when you called?

Chip fought sleep until he could no longer keep his eyes open. He rolled over and drifted off. He began to dream of chocolate chip cookies, fluffy white clouds, and speedy airplanes. He saw himself sitting in the seat of a large jet, munching on cookies and gazing out the window into the wispy, white clouds. The sky was a vibrant, brilliant shade of blue. As he glanced at the seat next to him, he noticed that it was empty. Mommy was not there, and neither was Daddy. Being without his parents would normally frighten him, but this time Chip felt amazingly calm. In fact, he felt empowered, like he was on some sort of a mission. He felt safe, protected, and not at all threatened. He didn't feel lost or abandoned—quite the opposite. He looked around the plane some more and noticed that it was totally empty. Chip was the only passenger. *That's strange.* Where was everybody? Where was he going?

"Attention, travelers," a woman's kind voice called out from the intercom. "We will be arriving soon. Please buckle your seat belts and prepare for landing. Next stop: heaven."

Heaven? Chip felt a sudden surge of excitement. Would he actually get to visit there? He thought only dead people and angels could go to heaven.

The plane slowly began its descent, and Chip could feel the change in the speed and the air. Everything felt lighter and dreamier, as if he were floating on a cottony cloud or a cushiony, giant marshmallow. "Wow, this is sooo cool!" he exclaimed.

"I thought you'd like it," a man's voice said.

Chip turned his head to see Connor now sitting next to him. Again, he was glowing white, with wavy, brown hair and kind, brown eyes. Connor grinned affectionately at the boy and softly patted him on the head.

"Hey, Connor!" Chip squealed with delight. "I tried to wait up for you, but I fell asleep. Where are we?"

"Well, I'm always visiting you, so this time I thought you might like to visit me." Connor smiled.

"In heaven?" Chip asked, his eyes wide with wonder.

"Yep, this is where I live."

"You live on a plane?"

"No, silly," he chuckled. "I live in heaven. It's all around you, and it's very beautiful. Why don't we go outside? I'll show you around."

"But I thought only God and Jesus and dead people and angels lived in heaven. Regular people can't go there. Why I am here?"

"Well, you're right that heaven is for those who are in spirit. But sometimes, a few lucky, special people get to catch a glimpse of heaven," Connor explained, winking. "They can't stay, of course, but they can visit for a bit."

"Awesome! Let's go!" Chip screamed, jumping from his seat. "I can't wait to see your home!"

He bolted for the plane door, and Connor helped him out. Once outside, breathtaking scenery and lush, green landscape surrounded them. Many trees stood tall and prominently, and the grass was greener than Chip had ever seen in his life. To the right was a beautiful, sparkling stream with two mallard ducks—one male and one female—floating by. As Chip scanned his surroundings, he saw a red fox dart out from behind the trees and zoom by him. He heard the whistling tunes of many varieties of birds, and he saw thousands of monarch butterflies filling the air like raindrops. Of course, the sky was that same shade of vibrant blue he had noticed from the airplane window, and the clouds were so white, they glowed. Everything was brighter, richer, and more vivid than it was on earth. And Chip felt happy, peaceful, and full of love. "Wow!" was all he could manage to say.

"Pretty amazing, huh?" Connor grinned.

They walked for a bit, stopping along the way to admire beautiful rose gardens, two adorable white-tailed deer fawns grazing, and a cardinal busily building a nest. They stopped near a crystal-clear stream.

Chip bent down to pick up some rocks and skipped them across the water. He also gathered tiny twigs, placed them carefully in the stream, and watched in awe as they floated away. Connor joined in the fun, and the two laughed and smiled like father and son enjoying an outdoor adventure. "I've got a surprise for you," Connor said. "Follow me, and I'll show you."

Chip's eyes were bright with wonder and curiosity as Connor led him to a serene lake surrounded by various kinds of lush, green trees. There was a dock at the lake's edge, with a small boat. When Chip saw it, his face lit up. "Do we get to go on that?" he asked eagerly.

"Yes, we do!" Connor replied enthusiastically. "And there's more, too. Just wait and see."

He took Chip's hand and helped him climb aboard. He pulled out a life jacket and made sure the boy was comfortable and secure. He started the boat's motor, and the two went out on the lake. Connor looked at Chip and gave him a big smile. The sweet, young child was beaming. He was so happy and excited to be going for a boat ride. Little did he know that the fun had just begun.

After a few minutes, Connor stopped the boat in the middle of the lake. It was very quiet and peaceful. He took out a fishing rod, put a worm on it, and began fishing. Within a few minutes, he reeled in a nice bluegill. He explained to Chip how to do it and let him try. With his strong hands gently guiding the boy, they soon felt a tug on the rod. "Did I catch something? Did I get a fish?" Chip asked eagerly.

"Let's see," Connor replied, helping him to reel it in.

Chip was proud to see another nice bluegill at the end of the line. "I did it! I caught my first fish!"

Connor patted him on the head and gave him a huge smile. "I'm proud of you," he said.

"I wish my Dad would do things like this with me," Chip said with a hint of sadness in his voice.

"Why don't you ask him?" Connor suggested. "He would probably like that."

"Well, he's always too busy with work. I don't know if he has time."

"Every father has time for his son," Connor said encouragingly. "But sometimes they lose sight of what's most important in life. Your job is to remind him. Make him remember what it's like to be a kid again. Help him to have fun and not work so hard. Take care of him. Do nice things for him."

"But what about Mommy? Who will take care of her?"

"Don't worry about your mom," Connor said. "I've got her covered."

"Are you her angel, too?"

"Absolutely! I will always be there for her."

"That's good to know, because Daddy isn't there for her much. And she seems sad. I want her to be happy."

"Don't worry, I've got that one covered too!" he assured Chip.

The two continued fishing for a while, enjoying the breathtaking scenery and the stillness of the lake. They reveled in the present moment—no worries, no thoughts, no pressure, and no sense of urgency. They soon accumulated a nice bucket of fish and decided to head back to shore.

Connor docked the boat, helped Chip get out, and

picked up their bucket of fish. "Now it's time for dinner," he announced. "Hang on to me tight, close your eyes, and count to ten."

Chip did as Connor asked. He could feel them being lifted off the ground and flying swiftly through the air. When he got to the number ten, they were no longer moving. He opened his eyes and saw a nice tan cape cod with a deck and barbecue grill outside. Like the lake, it was a peaceful setting, surrounded by many trees.

"Is this your house?" Chip asked.

"Yes, it is."

"You have houses in heaven?"

"Chip, in heaven, you can have, be, or do anything you want as long as it's in line with God's nature and your soul's purpose. Everything here is done with love and kindness."

"Wow! Heaven is a magical place. Can you have pets here too? I always wanted a puppy."

"Funny you should mention that," Connor said, smiling. "I was just about to introduce you to someone." An orangish-tan dog, a golden retriever, came trotting out of the woods, happily wagging his tail. Connor bent down and pet the dog. "This is my dog," he said. "His name is Buddy."

Chip bent over to pet him, and the dog affectionately licked the back of his hand.

"See, he likes you," Connor said. "Now I need to get dinner ready. You and Buddy can play for a bit while I cook."

Chip and the dog engaged in a little game of fetch with some sticks. Connor cleaned and seasoned the fish and began grilling them. The smell of tasty fish filled the air, and a pleasant breeze refreshed them.

When the meal was ready, Connor served the fish along with grilled asparagus and baked potatoes. Connor and Chip sat at a small picnic table outside on the wooden deck, and Buddy the pooch nibbled fish at their feet. They all enjoyed each other's company and a good, freshly grilled meal.

As the sun began to set, it was clear that it was time to go. "I want you to give your mom something from me," Connor said seriously.

"Okay," Chip agreed.

"It's something that belongs to her that she lost a very long time ago," he explained. "It will make her happy to see it again. Open your hand." Connor placed something shiny in the center of the boy's tiny, warm hand, gently closing it around the item. He gave Chip a hug and then slowly faded from view as his voice trailed off: "Tell your mom I love her…"

❉ ❉ ❉

As the sweet boy snoozed in his bed, rain gently tapped against the window and on the roof above him. The mellow, rhythmic sound filled the room, creating a soothing background that beckoned Chip to fall into an even deeper slumber.

Several hours later Chip felt a hand touch his forehead. A peek of sunlight was coming through his bedroom window, but he could still hear the pitter-patter of tiny raindrops. As he opened his eyes, he squinted to see who it was. Celeste was standing over him, smiling.

"Hiya, Mommy!"

"Good morning, sweetheart! Did you sleep well?"

"I slept great!"

"Rain sometimes helps us sleep better," she said, giving him a soft kiss on the forehead. "It's kind of like nature's lullaby."

"Can you open my curtains, please?" Chip asked.

"Sure," Celeste replied, letting the morning light shower into the room. "Oh, look. There's a rainbow."

"It's so pretty," Chip said as he gazed out his window at the mesmerizing colors.

"When I was a child, I used to think that rainbows were a sign of hope and a reminder of God's love for us," Celeste said. "And whenever I would see rays of light peeking through the clouds, I thought it meant God was speaking to me."

"What do you think now, Mommy?" her son asked.

Celeste paused before answering. So much of life was uncertain, confusing, and mysterious. After all these years, she still didn't understand how the world actually worked. Just when she thought she had it all figured out, something happened to test her faith or alter her view of reality. She didn't know what to think anymore. "I don't know," she answered finally.

"I do," said Chip confidently. "Rainbows are a peek at heaven." He remembered his dream of Connor and how he had visited the spirit world. He could still see the gorgeous scenery and the vivid colors. It was the ultimate place of beauty, peace, and love. It was paradise. He imagined himself being there again, surrounded by pure love. Chip even thought he could still feel the small, hard object that Connor had placed in the palm of his hand. *Wait a minute…* This wasn't his imagination. The ring was actually there! He really did visit with Connor last night! It wasn't a dream after all! A huge grin spread across his face as he thought of how happy Mommy would soon be. He was sure she would be thrilled to receive Connor's special gift.

"What's that big smile for?" Celeste asked. "What are you up to?"

"Nothing. I just have something for you. Open your hand and close your eyes."

"Oh?" she asked, puzzled, but doing as her son had asked.

Chip opened his little hand and placed the object into his mother's outstretched hand. "Okay, now you can open your eyes and look," Chip directed.

As she looked down, her heart did a sudden flip-flop. There in her palm was a heart-shaped ruby ring that Connor had given her years ago on Valentine's Day. She had lost it in the woods on a walk one day in the park. She had been pregnant with Chip at the time and needed some fresh air and time to think. She remembered how upset she was that she had misplaced it. The ring was very special to her—even more so, now. Tears began streaming down her face, and she smiled the biggest smile Chip had seen in a very long time.

"Mommy, why are you crying and smiling both? Are you happy or sad?"

"I'm overjoyed," Celeste said, wiping away the tears with the back of her hand. "Where did you find this?"

"In heaven."

"C'mon Chip, tell me the truth."

"An angel gave it to me."

"Please don't joke about this, Chip," Celeste said seriously. "Did you find this outside somewhere? In the park?"

"Yep, definitely outside somewhere, near some pretty trees," he replied, beaming with joy as he remembered how astonishing heaven looked.

"Wow, I'm surprised it stayed there all these years. That's really strange. Thank you so much for finding it for me! This ring is very special to Mommy."

"You're welcome," Chip smiled proudly, giving her a big bear hug. "Oh…by the way…*he* loves you!"

"I love you too, sweetie!" she said, kissing his forehead.

Mommy didn't quite get it. But she was happy, and that was all that mattered. Someday she would come to know the truth. Connor would be sure to visit her, too, and let her know just how loved and protected she really was.

CHAPTER 7
KISS FROM A ROSE

*F*all and winter passed quickly, and Celeste was thankful for the arrival of spring. She loved the sweet fragrance of the flowering trees and the delicate pastel colors that surrounded the houses in her neighborhood. She always looked forward to spring because it signified new life. Everything was revived after being dormant throughout the cold winter months. Spring gave Celeste a sense of hope and brightened her mood, which had definitely been much needed since Connor's passing.

Dave had been living in their house for several months now, despite his outrage and disbelief at Celeste's paranormal experiences with Connor. He had encouraged her to go to see their therapist with him again, but there was nothing really wrong with Celeste. She showed some signs of mild depression. Otherwise, she was a healthy, normal woman going through ordinary struggles and emotions. She wasn't delusional, and there was no evidence of any serious mental illness. The therapist urged Dave to be patient and understanding with his wife, since she was clearly grieving the loss of someone important to her. She also asked him to please consider the possibility that Celeste really did have some sort of a guardian angel watching over her.

"It's a *good* thing," the therapist said to both of them during their last session. "There are so many unknown and unseen forces in this world. We may not understand them, but we must never dismiss them. Just enjoy the miracle and feel blessed."

Celeste did indeed feel blessed! She enjoyed the many songs and signs that kept Connor alive in her heart. When something that reminded her of him came into her life, she was always filled with such comfort, peace, and joy.

On the other hand, Dave made her increasingly uncomfortable and uneasy. She did have love for him, but it was more like a brotherly love. Dave didn't truly understand her or know her. He had long assumed that she had the same interests and goals that he did and expected her to agree with his ideas and life philosophy. But Celeste couldn't embrace his beliefs or lifestyle. Dave lived primarily in the material world. He mistakenly believed that he could show his family love and affection with what he could give them. Celeste, on the other hand, knew the only way to truly love was with your whole heart and your entire being. This couldn't be accomplished with a fancy job title, an elaborate home, or lavish gifts; it could only be done when you completely surrendered your heart to another person. Love wasn't about objects and things; it was about people and feelings. That was one thing Celeste was sure of.

Dave didn't quite understand love in the same way Celeste did, but he was smart and an excellent problem solver—traits that she had always admired in him. He seemed to know what to do in every situation. He was organized, meticulous, and a remarkable planner. He excelled at analyzing data and coming to conclusions about what steps to take to get a positive outcome.

Celeste had once believed that these attributes would enable Dave to help her sort out her feelings and the strange occurrences related to Connor. She now knew that Dave would be of no help in that department. He laughed at her whenever she brought it up. It's not that he was being intentionally unkind. He just didn't fully believe in or embrace angels, spirit communication, or the afterlife—all of which had become a prominent part of Celeste's life. Since he had never witnessed or experienced contact from someone who had died, he found the whole idea preposterous and highly unlikely. So Celeste stopped talking about Connor and the signs. Dave never seemed very interested anyway and was clearly always intensely jealous of her never-ending love for her deceased former boyfriend.

Although Celeste and Dave had tried hard to work out their differences, they were on totally different wavelengths now. They lived together and slept in the same bed, but they were often worlds apart. They were cordial to each other. They showed each other affection.

They even made love occasionally, but it was more out of obligation than feelings. Despite the growing distance between them, their family life was secure. And, of course, everything was great financially. Dave was working hard as usual and providing for them. They occasionally shared meals, family outings, and rare vacations with Chip. But although Celeste technically had a man to depend on again, something was still missing in her life. She needed something more. She needed something deeper and more fulfilling. She needed Connor.

Celeste still couldn't seem to get him out of her mind, no matter how hard she tried. And despite many months of thinking, reading, and searching, she had not unveiled the reason for the unusual happenings in her life since he had died. The steady stream of coincidences had continued. She was still seeing lots of repeating numbers, such as "111," "1111," and "444." She noticed these numbers on license plates, clocks, store receipts, e-mail time stamps, and more. She also heard Pink Floyd songs everywhere she went. She overheard Connor's first name in conversations in shopping centers, on television, and on the radio. She saw trucks with his name on them, such as those from Connor's Home Improvement and Connor's Florist. It seemed that everywhere she went, there was some reminder of him.

As bizarre as it was, Celeste still didn't understand why these things were happening to her. Despite the overwhelming evidence that Connor was around her, sometimes creeping doubts entered her mind. Was he really reaching out to her from beyond? She still wondered sometimes if maybe she was causing these incidents because he was on her mind. It was certainly possible that all of these occurrences were coming from her, not him. Or maybe she was just noticing things that reminded her of him because she missed him. That didn't explain the dream her son Chip had had about the angel that fit Connor's description, or the sensation of someone snuggling behind her in bed.

Her husband had been quick to point out numerous times that Celeste really didn't have any concrete proof of anything. Hearing a song or finding a chunk of mud on her sleeve didn't prove Connor's spirit lived on or that he was visiting Celeste. Both could easily be explained as just simple coincidences. Like Dave had said, Connor never appeared in front of her or spoke to her. It's true she had thought she heard his voice warning her to pay attention while driving, but that could have just been her own instincts. Her husband always had a reasonable, logical explanation for everything. He refused to believe there was anything supernatural going on. However, no matter what he said or how he attempted to explain away everything that had happened to her, Celeste still felt that there was more to it.

She still needed to know the truth. She needed to know what exactly was going on and why. If it was Connor, then she should be able to ask him to give her something specific that she couldn't possibly create on her own. Not a song; something more concrete, something more tangible. Something like the heart-shaped chunk of mud. Only this time, she had to be certain it wasn't just a fluke. This was the only way she could finally have undeniable proof of his continued existence and his angelic visits. She decided to give her idea a try. After all, what did she have to lose?

"Connor, I want you to send me a rose. But I want to know for sure that it's meant for me and not just a coincidence," Celeste explained. "Please send me just a rose." She paused for a moment before deciding on a color. Red was too common and cliché. White was too plain. Yellow was meant for friends, but he was more than just a friend to her. Lavender was too rare. "A pink one," she decided finally.

A couple of hours later, Celeste was browsing through an advertisement for the department store, Kohl's, when something fell out. It was a perfume sample card. She picked it up and glanced at it. It was a cologne called Someday. The cap of the bottle was a *pink rose* with a red heart in the center of it! *Could this be my sign?* Celeste wondered. It was indeed a pink rose, and the name of the cologne was the same as the song she had kept hearing right after Connor passed. The words to the song echoed in her head, and she again wondered what his plan was to help her.

"Connor, if you have truly been around me, sending me signs and songs, when and how are you going to make things all right? You can't magically come back to life. We can't go back and change the past. So how do you propose you'll help me?"

Celeste glanced down at the perfume ad again and gazed at the red heart in the center of the pink rose. If this was from Connor, it certainly was very sweet and did get her attention. But maybe she was just *looking* for a pink rose. It's possible she had noticed it because a pink rose was on her mind. That must be it! Celeste decided it was probably just another coincidence. And even if it wasn't, she wanted more. She wanted better. This was not the unmistakable, undeniable proof that she was looking for. As interesting as it was, it just wasn't enough to make her believe.

"Connor, that's pretty weak," she said aloud as she tossed the perfume ad into the garbage. She challenged him to do better. If Connor could hear her and really was trying to communicate, then he should be able to give her a stronger, more convincing sign, shouldn't he?

Over the next few days, Celeste saw pink roses in a few places. One of her Facebook friends changed her profile picture to a pink rose. Then another did the same. She also saw a bumper sticker with a pink rose on someone's car while she was stuck in traffic one day. But these things weren't enough to convince her. They could all just be random coincidences.

Then one day Celeste was reading some posts on a women's forum she frequently visited. Someone made reference to a poem about a rose and provided a link to it. Celeste clicked on the link and read the poem. It talked about how the dew on rose petals is symbolic of the tears we cry for those who have passed away. As she scrolled down to the bottom of the poem, there was a large picture of a *pink rose!* Then she noticed the date when the poem was originally written: May 11, 2006. A chill ran down her spine. *That's Connor's birthday, seven years ago!* she thought.

Celeste was starting to think that maybe this was her sign from Connor. It was a pink rose *and* mentioned his birthday. What were the chances of that? And, she had been a member of these forums for over a year now and hadn't seen this poem or the pink rose photo before.

She still couldn't be 100 percent sure, but decided she probably couldn't get a sign much better than that. Connor was dead, after all. He certainly couldn't just go to the store, buy her a pink rose, and deliver it to her in person. Asking a spirit for a flower would be like asking the wind to deliver a newspaper right to her doorstep. It wasn't easy for something or someone without physical form to deliver a physical object. What was she thinking? She had expected far too much from him. And, he was doing everything he could to give it to her. First with the perfume ad, then the roses that appeared on her friends' profiles, next the bumper sticker, and now this.

Celeste realized how frustrating it must be for Connor to try over and over again to get through to her. Each time she dismissed his efforts and always wanted more. Luckily Connor was patient and refused to give up on her.

Finally satisfied that the rose poem and picture with Connor's birthday were from him, Celeste decided to stop watching for a pink rose. She kept busy with work and taking care of Chip. About a week later, she was feeling stressed and exhausted, so she decided it was time for a vacation. She wanted to spend more time with her son and longed to be outside enjoying the spring weather instead of being cooped up in the office. Dave was too busy and not interested in a trip, so Celeste requested a week off without him.

She packed suitcases for herself and Chip and set off for the gorgeous Pocono Mountains. A couple of times during their travels, she thought she saw her abusive ex-boyfriend, Andy, in the distance, following her in his shiny, red Corvette. She decided finally that she must just be feeling stressed and imagining it was him. Even after all these years, the painful memories and images of their volatile relationship haunted her. She wondered if she would ever really escape from her tormented past. Somehow it was still very much a part of her, always lurking just below the surface. She was certain this vacation was just what she and Chip needed. She longed to get away from it all, to leave her fears and troubles behind. A trip to the Poconos would be the perfect opportunity to do just that.

A few hours later, Celeste and Chip arrived at a cozy cabin not far from a state park. Celeste carried in their luggage and looked around at the knotty-pine interior. The cabin was small, but comfortably decorated in rich shades of blue and forest green. It had a rich, earthy smell that made Celeste feel immediately at home. Chip seemed to like it, too, and carefully placed his favorite teddy bear on his bed. Then he was ready to get their vacation started. "Mommy, Mommy, can we go to the park now and eat? I'm hungry!"

"Of course, sweetie!"

Chip was so excited and couldn't wait to have a picnic lunch. He had talked about a picnic all morning. Celeste locked up the cabin, and they jumped back into the car to head to the corner store. The mountains created a majestic backdrop to the picture-perfect scenery. There were lots of trees, especially pines, and the air had a fresh, crisp smell to it. It was invigorating and refreshing. In just a few short minutes, Celeste had stopped at the corner store and picked up some bread, cheddar cheese, and turkey lunch meat. Then they set off for the park.

They found a gorgeous spot to eat on a hill overlooking some pine trees. There was a picnic table sitting at the top of the hill, as if it was meant for them. It was the perfect location for their lunch. As Celeste was about to sit down on the bench, something caught her eye on the ground underneath it. She reached down to pick it up, and was amazed to find it was a *pink rose* made of silk!

The familiar tingly sensation ran through her body, and Celeste was filled with an overwhelming sense of love, joy, and peace. For a minute, she thought she could feel Connor right there beside her. As a warm, gentle breeze caressed her skin, she imagined his breath on her neck. Time stood still. She could almost feel his lips on her skin, giving her soft kisses. This rose surely must be from Connor! There is no way she could have caused this to happen. It was so unexpected and miraculous. Her mind couldn't possibly have created this on its own. And besides, she wasn't even looking for a pink rose anymore. It wasn't even on her mind. She was certain that this rose was a precious, beautiful gift from Connor. Somehow he had moved heaven and earth to get this rose to her—the pink rose she had asked for. For the first time in many months, Celeste was truly happy.

"What's that, Mom?" Chip asked.

"It's a pink rose," she replied, smiling. "And I think it's meant for me."

With tears in her eyes, she whispered: "Thank you, Connor!" She would never again doubt him or the experiences she had. Connor was definitely communicating with her in the most amazing way.

"See, I told you he loves you," Chip said.

"Who?"

"Connor. He told me so. The day he gave me your ring."

"What?" Celeste asked, stunned. "What do you mean, he *gave* you the ring? I thought you found it outside in the park."

"I told you, I got it from heaven. I told you an angel gave it to me. But you didn't believe me."

"Connor actually *gave* you my ring?"

"Yes, and he said to tell you he loves you."

"When? How?"

"When I was sleeping one night, he took me on an airplane to heaven. It was so pretty! It looked like a really cool park with lots of trees, butterflies, flowers, and animals. We went for a ride on his boat. We went fishing. And, I met his dog, Buddy. Then he gave me the ring to give to you."

Celeste paused for few moments to absorb what her son was telling her. It all seemed so unbelievable. The only explanation that made sense was that Chip had had a dream about all of this. But Connor did indeed have a golden retriever named Buddy, who had died about ten years ago. Chip didn't know any of that. And how would a dream explain what her son was telling her about the ring? He said Connor *gave* it to him. The ring was real, and she was wearing it right now. Did Connor actually take her son to heaven somehow? How was that even possible? It was just too difficult to comprehend.

The world was full of so many unknowns, so many unexplained events. At one time Celeste would have been certain her son was making this all up or that it was just a dream. But in her heart and soul, she believed him.

She didn't know how any of this was possible, but it felt true. It felt right. And if Chip could visit Connor somehow, maybe she could, too! That thought filled her with such hope and excitement that she wanted to see him right then.

"Mommy, do you believe me now?" Chip asked.

"Yes, sweetie, I do."

"Good, because when you picked up the flower a few minutes ago, he was here. I felt him pat my head, just like he did that night he gave me the ring. I couldn't see him. But I know he was here to give you that flower. 'Cause he loves you. He is your angel, too."

"Maybe he is," Celeste agreed.

Her son flashed her a big smile full of happiness and relief. "Mommy, this is the best vacation ever!"

"Why do you say that?" she asked, although she had to admit that she totally agreed with her son.

"Because Connor is here with us," Chip replied. "We're on vacation with an angel! That is so awesome!"

Celeste smiled radiantly. A gentle breeze brushed across her cheek. For a moment she actually thought she could feel him again. "I have an idea, Chip," she said. "Let's go fishing! How would you like to catch your first fish?"

"Um, Mommy," Chip began, feeling a bit guilty. "I want to go fishing. But...there's just one thing...I already caught my first fish."

"What do you mean? Daddy and I never took you fishing."

"I went with Connor, remember? In heaven that night."

"Oh, yeah, right." She smiled. "I forgot. I guess he

beat me to it."

"Sorry, Mommy," Chip apologized.

"No, sweetie. It's okay. I'm glad Connor taught you how to fish. I'm happy your first experience was with him. Let's go. I packed some fishing rods and supplies in the trunk."

They soon had everything they needed and were enjoying the afternoon fishing together. Celeste was amazed at how good Chip was at it. He explained each step and knew exactly what he was doing. It did really seem like someone had already taught him. Ironically, that person was supposed to be dead. She never imagined in her wildest dreams that her deceased former boyfriend would be the one to teach her son how to fish. The world really was a bizarre and interesting place!

After their fishing excursion, Celeste and her son headed back to the cabin for a delicious dinner of pan-fried trout with lemon, accompanied by green beans and Tater Tots. They also played games: Candy Land, Memory, and Go Fish. They ended their day with a nice bedtime story: *Oh, the Places You'll Go!* by Dr. Seuss. It was always one of Chip's favorites.

That night mother and son slept soundly in their cozy cabin. The windows were open slightly, so fresh air filled the place and created the perfect environment for a restful slumber. Their vacation spot was quiet and peaceful. There were no sounds of cars rushing by or radios blaring, only the soothing chirps of crickets.

Celeste soon found herself deep in a dream. She was looking out the cabin's living room window at the stunning, blue sky filled with thousands of fluffy, white clouds. As she admired the beauty, her eyes fixed upon an unusually shaped cloud. She blinked—she couldn't believe her eyes. It was in the shape of a rose. The petals were clearly defined. The only part missing was the stem. Was this another gift from Connor? *I need to get a camera and take a picture quickly*, she thought. *Then maybe Dave will believe that all this stuff is real and not just a figment of my imagination!*

She ran to her bedroom to get a camera, but when she returned, the rose was gone. Disappointed, she set the camera on the oak end table and stood there in silence.

Suddenly Connor was standing there in front of her. He looked extra handsome and radiant. He was younger than he had been when he died by about ten years. He looked to be in his mid-twenties. His eyes were brighter, his smile was irresistible, and he was surrounded by a white, glowing light. Celeste felt like he was really there with her. So many thoughts and emotions flooded her mind. She was overcome with feelings of joy, love, sadness, longing, and regret. There was so much she wanted to say to him, so many things she wanted him to know. Most important, she yearned to apologize for leaving him, for not trying to be a part of his life after he moved away, and for never telling him that she loved him.

As she and Connor faced each other, she gazed into his eyes, her own eyes brimming with tears. "I'm so sorry," she said softly, ready to tell him of all of her regrets and mistakes. She was hoping he would forgive her.

Connor didn't utter a word. He just looked at her, his warm, brown eyes reflecting compassion and understanding. Then he simply took her in his arms and gave her a tender, loving kiss on the lips. Celeste got the feeling that everything was okay with them. Although he didn't say anything, she felt like he was communicating that there was nothing to forgive. He wasn't upset or angry with her. He loved her. She could feel his love embracing her and giving her comfort. No words were needed. Then he slowly faded from view, until he was completely gone.

Celeste woke up the next morning with the distinct feeling that she had just spent time with Connor. Was that just a dream, or did he actually come to visit her last night? She didn't know the answer to that question. All she knew was how she felt—safe, loved, protected, and forgiven. Somehow that was enough for her.

CHAPTER 8
LET'S DO LUNCH

*B*eing away from the crowds, traffic, and the hustle of daily life was rejuvenating for Celeste. She enjoyed being out in nature and spending some quality time with her son. It was hard to return home after such a peaceful week. She did see a noticeable improvement in her mood after the trip, in part because of the vacation itself and in part because of her experiences with Connor. The rose and her dream with him left her feeling hopeful and took away some of her sadness.

After a restful week with her son, she returned to work relaxed, refreshed, and ready for whatever was next in her life. She was busy crunching numbers at the office when the phone rang. She was surprised and delighted to hear her old friend Sue's voice. Sue was the one who had helped arrange the blind date between her and Connor.

"Hey, chickie," said Sue enthusiastically. "I haven't seen you in almost a year! Are you free for lunch? We have some catching up to do!" A lunch invitation was a welcome distraction from Celeste's mundane work morning, and she gladly accepted. She had so much to tell Sue! She grabbed her purse and headed over to Lou's Deli. She could really go for a roasted turkey-and-avocado sandwich and a cup of broccoli-cheddar soup.

As Celeste arrived in the restaurant parking lot, she saw Sue pulling in. The girl was still drop-dead gorgeous. Even through the car window, Celeste could see her perfectly groomed, shiny brown hair glistening in the sunlight. Sue waved frantically as she parked the car. She got out quickly and ran to Celeste to give her a big, warm hug. "I've missed you, girl!" she exclaimed.

"I've missed you too, Sue. Life was always so much more interesting and exciting when we hung out." Celeste grinned, remembering how Sue was always up for something wild and crazy.

She recalled the time Sue had convinced her to do shots of tequila and dance on stage in some bar. The next day Celeste hardly remembered what had happened, but the pictures sure were hilarious! There were several of the two of them puckering up for the camera and posing like models. There were also a few with some guys with their arms around the girls. Definitely out of character for Celeste! In fact, it was a rare occasion to find Celeste drunk. She was always so guarded and in control of herself and her feelings. It took a lot to get her to let loose and just have fun.

Sue, on the other hand, always knew how to have a good time. Celeste looked forward to hearing about her friend's life and her latest adventures.

The two women placed their orders and waited at the counter for their lunch to be ready. Luckily the restaurant wasn't very crowded yet, so it didn't take too long. Soon they were sitting down in a nice booth next the window, munching on their sandwiches as they eagerly chatted about their lives. "So, what's new with you?" Celeste asked curiously. She wondered what kind of trouble Sue had gotten herself into lately.

"Well, you're not going to believe this, but...I'm getting married!" Sue said excitedly, flashing a big, marquise-style diamond solitaire.

"Oh, Sue! Congratulations! That is so exciting! I didn't know you were even dating anyone seriously," said Celeste, prompting her friend for details.

"Yeah, I know. I always said I never wanted to be tied down or get married. I thought that would make life too boring," said Sue. "But Tim...he's different! He's an amazing guy. So kind, loving, thoughtful. And he's good in bed, too!"

As Sue talked about her fiancé, her green eyes lit up, and Celeste's once wild-and-crazy friend was transformed into a gentle, dreamy schoolgirl. She really was in love! Celeste had never seen her like this before. "I'm so happy for you," Celeste said sincerely. "I can tell you're really into this guy."

"I am. Definitely. He's a perfect match for me," Sue said beaming.

"That's wonderful that you found the right man for you," said Celeste. "My track record, on the other hand, hasn't been so great."

Sue's face suddenly turned serious. "Oh, by the

way," she said with a hint of hesitation. "My cousin called me and was asking about you."

"Andy? I hope he's not still obsessed with me!"

"Well, Celeste, you know my cousin has serious issues. He only calls me when he wants or needs something – like drug money, a ride, or advice. This time it was for advice. He wanted to know how to get you back."

"What did you tell him?"

"I told him that you're happily married and he needs to move on."

"Thanks," Celeste said, feeling relieved. "That man scares me. The thought of him trying to worm his way back into my life makes me shudder."

"I know, sweetie. Andy did some terrible things to you. He seriously needs help. I try to keep my distance from him as much as possible. So, tell me about you? How are you and Dave doing?"

"Well, not so great," Celeste said. "We separated for a while. We're just so different from each other. But then one day, he came back—and we had an amazing night together! I thought maybe things were going to be okay for us. Until I told him about Connor—"

"Wait a minute," Sue said interrupting. "You mean, *the* Connor? The blind-date hottie? Your ex-boyfriend? Are you guys shacking up?"

"No, we're not *shacking up*," Celeste said with an irritated tone. Her crystal-blue eyes began to fill with tears as she strained to tell her friend the sad and unfortunate news. "Connor died several months ago," she continued. "He was on his way home from Rome, and the plane crashed. He supposedly wanted to see me."

"Oh, Celeste. I'm so sorry," said Sue sadly, patting her friend's arm. "I always thought you two were really good together. I was surprised when you dumped him and he moved away. It just didn't seem right."

"Yeah, I know," sighed Celeste. "But the weirdest part about all of this is that I think Connor has been communicating with me from beyond the grave."

"What? That's so wild…and cool…and *creepy*. All at the same time!" Sue said, intrigued.

"So, you believe me?"

"Of course. Why wouldn't I?" Sue answered assuredly. "You've always been so practical and level-headed. If you think Connor's spirit is around you, then I totally believe you. Please, tell me more! I want to hear all the juicy details!"

Celeste explained the whole story to Sue. She told her about how it had started with the songs and signs. She explained how she had felt someone lie next to her in bed and how her son Chip had claimed to have seen an angel that same night who fit Connor's description exactly. She told her about the ring, the heart-shaped chunk of mud, and the mysterious pink rose she had found in the park. And finally she described her vivid dream.

"Wow, what a sweetheart and a romantic! To think he would do all of that for you even after he died—it's just incredible!" Sue said. "Connor always was a nice guy, and such a hottie! I would love having a hunky guardian angel like him hanging around me. So what are you going to do?"

"I don't know," said Celeste. "I need to understand more about why he's around me and what he wants."

"Well, that's easy, kiddo," said Sue knowingly. "He obviously loves you! And I can tell you love him, too. Too bad humans and spirits can't hook up. That would be one interesting relationship!"

"Okay, so even if he does love me, that still doesn't explain everything," said Celeste. "I mean, shouldn't he be in heaven, hanging out with angels and harps and God? Why is he here with me so much? Is he stuck or something?"

"Hmm. Good point. I hadn't thought of that," said Sue. "Have you considered seeing a psychic medium?"

"Dave would probably kill me!" Celeste exclaimed.

"And then you could be with Connor! Sounds like a win-win situation to me!" Sue joked.

"No. Seriously," said Celeste. "Dave doesn't like what's going on with Connor. He's jealous of my feelings for him and feels threatened in some way. He doesn't want to share my heart with another man, even if that man is dead. And besides, he doesn't believe in all that stuff anyway. He says it's all just coincidence and my imagination. He thinks communicating with the dead is a bunch of baloney."

"Well, Dave has to get a clue," Sue said. "That man works too much, is far too serious, and just not any fun! Are you sure you two actually had an amazing night? Is Dave even capable of that?"

"Well, I didn't think so. Until he came back and practically tore my clothes off right at the door," smirked Celeste. "He was so passionate."

"No way! Not the Dave I know! Are you sure it was really him?" Sue asked, laughing.

"Yes, it was him. He was all excited about his job

promotion, and he seemed really happy to see me."

"Oh, that explains it!" Sue said understandingly. "He was on some sort of adrenalin rush because of his promotion. Now it all makes sense!"

"So you think it was just a fluke?" Celeste asked, disappointed.

"Absolutely. How long have you been married?"

"Six years."

"And have you ever had a night like that with him before? Or since?"

"No."

"I rest my case."

"So what do you think I should do?" Celeste asked.

"Divorce Dave. Have a fling with the ghost," she joked. "Honestly, I really don't know, Celeste. But you do deserve to have fun. You need a man who can help you to take some risks, enjoy your life. You need a guy who accepts you for who you are and doesn't try to change you. Someone more like…"

"Connor," said Celeste, finishing Sue's sentence.

"Yeah. Does he have a brother?" she asked hopefully.

"No, just a sister."

"Is his sister hot?" asked Sue.

"Yes, but I am *not* into girls," said Celeste firmly.

"I know," said Sue, laughing. "Just trying to give you options. No, seriously, I was just kidding. You really need to lighten up. Dave is not good for you. He brings out the serious, uptight woman in you. At least with Connor, you could let down your hair and dance a little."

Celeste tugged on the back of her wavy, blonde

ponytail. She knew Sue was right. She and Connor may have been different, too, but they complemented each other perfectly. They brought out the best in each other. She and Dave, on the other hand, were dissimilar in a bad way. Their personalities clashed, and their differences caused conflicts and arguments. He never seemed to see her point of view. Dave didn't understand her. But still she loved, respected, and admired him. He was a good man and a great provider. He was ambitious. He was a hard worker. Her life with him was secure—just not passionate or exciting or inspiring. Did she really need excitement in her life? Wasn't being secure enough?

Celeste thought once again of the pink rose Connor had sent her. She remembered the heart-shaped chunk of mud and the thrill she got just knowing that he still cared about her. She recalled Dave's anger and jealousy over her fascination with Connor. Sue was right. Dave wasn't much fun. Something was definitely missing in her life. The only time she felt any passion or excitement lately was when Connor's spirit was around. She was always on some sort of high after hearing from him. She rarely felt that way with Dave. So what was she supposed to do about it? She certainly didn't want to just give up the life she had. Besides, Connor wasn't exactly available for a relationship anymore. And frankly, the thought of being alone scared her. So what was next for Celeste?

As she contemplated her choices, the words from the woman in her dream came into her mind again.

Your life's purpose is just what you choose to do
But your soul's purpose is for eternity.

Maybe her next task was to find her soul's purpose. Somehow life was leading her in a different direction than she had ever expected. But what exactly *was* her soul's purpose? And how could she find it?

CHAPTER 9
STEPPING STONES

*C*eleste had been feeling much less distressed and more at peace since finding the pink rose in the park and apologizing to Connor in her dream. Talking to Sue the other day had further solidified her beliefs and helped to convince her of her ex-boyfriend's everlasting love for her. It was comforting to know that Connor was truly alive in spirit form. He was reaching out to her, trying to communicate. And she thought it was all very touching and sweet!

But as she had explained to Sue, she didn't fully understand why he was still around her. She also couldn't escape the nagging feeling inside that there was something more she was supposed to do. What did he want her to know? What was he trying to tell her? Was their relationship unfinished or unsettled? Did he need her help? Was he trying to help her? She just had to find out the answers to these questions.

One night before bed, she decided to ask Connor directly for some answers. She spoke aloud to him: "If you have a message for me or need to tell me something, please send it to me in a dream." She went off to sleep, confident that she would understand everything in the morning.

But Connor never came during the night. There were no visits, no dreams of him, and no messages. Celeste awoke feeling sad and disappointed. She concluded that maybe he didn't have anything important to tell her, after all. Once again, all she was left with were questions.

"There's still something I want to show you."

Celeste heard the voice clearly in her head. Was Connor speaking to her? For a brief moment, she experienced a surge of hope. Then she thought of what her husband Dave had told her about how it could be coming from her own mind. *Maybe he's right.* She realized how far-fetched it all seemed. She didn't doubt Connor still existed in spirit form. She had received plenty of proof of that. But him actually being able to speak to her in her head seemed unlikely. *I must surely be losing it*, she thought. *Connor can't speak to me or show me anything. He's dead.*

She found it unlikely that a spirit could just take her somewhere and show her something while she was awake and fully conscious. He didn't have a body and wasn't her personal tour guide. Then again, what about that ring he had somehow given to Chip in a dream? Celeste felt frustrated and confused. Nothing seemed to make sense to her anymore. Her experiences defied logic. She was so full of questions. How could she find out what she needed to know? Why couldn't Connor just tell her?

Celeste needed to get out of the house. She was compelled to go for a walk to clear her head. So she got dressed quickly in a grey T-shirt and jeans and headed outside. Dave was still sleeping, and she knew Chip wouldn't be up for a while, either. It was a perfect time for a nice, long walk.

As she began her stroll, Celeste was instantly calmed. She breathed in the fresh, fragrant summer air and let nature soothe her. The sun was just coming up, so the sky was filled with breathtaking shades of orange and pink. It was a gorgeous morning!

She traveled through their neighborhood, letting her thoughts drift and her mind clear. She enjoyed the warm glow of sunrise and the way it cast brilliant shadows on the landscape. Celeste wondered where Connor was and what the scenery looked like there. She imagined that heaven would be filled with so much beauty and wonder. But if it was so spectacular there, then why was he hanging around here? And why didn't he visit her in a dream last night?

Her thoughts were interrupted when she thought she spotted Andy hiding among the trees. A second glance revealed nothing. No one was there. Why did her abusive ex haunt her like that? She had tried to leave him and her past behind, but sometimes, when she least expected it, Andy popped up again. Occasionally he appeared in her mind and thoughts, but other times, she briefly thought she saw him in the neighborhood or on the road she traveled. Even though they hadn't been together for several years, he still had some kind of weird power and control over her. He still frightened her. She often felt she must watch her back in case he tried to weasel his way back into her life. She shuddered at that disturbing thought!

It wasn't the time or place for Andy's unwelcome intrusion. Celeste had enough on her mind. She was determined to release her thoughts and concentrate instead on enjoying her walk. She shifted her focus to the scenery around her and the sensation of the gentle morning breeze brushing against her skin. She loved the feeling of peace and freedom she experienced while outside. It brought her much-needed comfort and lifted her spirits.

As Celeste turned the corner, she almost stepped on something on the sidewalk in front of her and stopped abruptly in her tracks. There on the path beneath her was the biggest, most beautiful monarch butterfly she had ever seen. It was at least six inches across. Celeste stood there staring at it, entranced by its beauty. The butterfly gently opened and closed its wings, as if it were waving hello to her. Time stood still as she watched the insect in awe, and she was filled with love and peace.

After a few minutes, the butterfly gently flapped its wings and slowly coasted up into the sky. She watched as it climbed higher and higher, up past the tops of the tallest trees. Celeste just stood there in amazement, observing this magnificent bug. She was surprised at how high it had traveled and expected it to stop soon. But it didn't. The remarkable insect drifted higher and higher, way up into the clouds, until it finally disappeared. It was as if that butterfly had traveled straight up to heaven. She suddenly remembered the words she had heard this morning right after waking:

There's still something I want to show you.

"Was this what Connor wanted to show me?" Celeste wondered.

Again a voice came into her head and said: "I want you to know what is possible."

Celeste had to admit she hadn't thought a monarch butterfly could grow so large or fly so high. She was pleasantly surprised by the discovery. But she still didn't know exactly what Connor was trying to tell her. It's true that her beliefs about monarch butterflies had been changed by the incident. She found out that a butterfly could fly high up into the clouds, higher than she ever saw a bird soar. That was definitely something she never dreamed was possible. But what did that have to do with Connor or her? Did he want her to realize that the impossible was possible? Did he want her to know that her views about reality weren't necessarily accurate?

She needed to understand. But even more than that, she ached to be with him in some way. Every fiber of her being was drawn to him like a magnet. It didn't matter that he was physically dead. The strength and vitality of his spirit were more powerful than any being living on earth. There were times when she thought she could feel his presence. But she never knew for sure what was her imagination and what was real. It was so hard to separate fantasy from reality.

She did believe that, at times, he really was watching over her, reaching out to her and trying to make his presence known. Connor wanted her to know that he was with her sometimes. He needed her to understand that life really was eternal. He wanted her to have faith and believe in a power greater than herself. He was still strong. He was still protective of her. And he obviously still cared about her. Why else would he do these things?

Unless. Uh-oh. Celeste suddenly had a disturbing thought. She had mentioned the idea to Sue just the other day, but now it seemed even more serious. Maybe Connor was really stuck. She had heard about purgatory and about earthbound souls who hadn't yet crossed over into the light. She had read stories about spirits who hung around earth because they had unfinished business or didn't know how to get to heaven. Or those who had not done enough to earn entry into the pearly gates. Was Connor imprisoned here? Did he need her help to get to the other side? Was he not at peace?

Now more than ever, she needed to find out why he was around her. She had to make sure he was not distressed or trapped between two worlds. She needed to know why all of this was happening. Celeste had no idea how to answer these questions on her own. She had tried for months, all to no avail. So she decided to do the only other thing left: consult a professional. Celeste had to help Connor. And she was willing to risk her marriage and her relationship with Dave to do so. *Who cares what Dave thinks!*

She raced home, ran in the front door, and sat down at her computer. Into a search engine, she typed the words "spirit communication." She found several entries, including a few local researchers and psychic mediums. One in particular caught her attention. Celeste clicked on the link. It read: "Star Walker, spirit traveler and afterlife expert."

As seen in her photos, Star was a middle-aged woman with curly, reddish-orange hair and crystal-blue eyes. Her skin was a powdery white, and she radiated joy and peace. *She looks familiar,* Celeste thought. *But where have I seen her before?*

Star's website had pictures of stars and a bridge that glowed with a golden light. Star claimed she not only could communicate with the dead, but had developed a technique for traveling to the spirit world. According to the website, this woman could somehow cause a bridge to materialize in the physical world. This bridge could then be crossed by the living, where they could visit with the dead. It sounded so unbelievable, like something out of a science fiction or fantasy novel, but somehow Celeste was intrigued. Her intuition told her that this was the woman who would help her. Celeste picked up the phone and dialed the number.

"Star Walker here," said a kind, gentle voice.

"Um, hello…I want to set up an appointment," Celeste said nervously.

"Yes, Celeste," the woman replied. "I have been expecting you."

"How did you know my name?" Celeste asked.

"Don't you remember, dear?" Star asked. "We've met before."

"Your picture did look familiar, but I don't recall ever meeting you—" Celeste stopped abruptly. Suddenly she saw flashes of a dream. The woman in the office who was helping her spell words was Star! She was also the woman who had educated her on the difference between her life's purpose and her soul's purpose!

"Were you in my dreams?" Celeste asked.

"You do remember!" Star exclaimed. "Yes, I was helping you to learn the truth. I travel to the spirit world and can also travel into people's dreams to deliver important messages. He is very much alive, Celeste. He's around you quite often. The songs, the signs, the voices in your head. That is how he tries to reach you."

"That's what I wanted to know for sure," Celeste said. "I also want to be certain that he is okay. I want him to be happy and at peace. But I don't understand why he is around me so much. Is he stuck on earth? Does he need help to get to heaven?"

"No, he is here because he chooses to be. He wants to help you. He is doing very well. And, to answer your next question: yes, you can," Star said.

"You mean I can reach him somehow? I can actually see him and communicate with him directly?" Celeste asked.

"Absolutely. Those who pass are closer than we think. They always want to communicate with us, but they have trouble, because we often dismiss the signs they send as imagination or coincidence," Star explained. "Know that what you've been encountering is very real. Trust it. Believe. Let go. Know that the impossible is possible."

"I'll certainly try. Although I must say, it is hard to believe in something you can't see or touch," Celeste admitted.

Celeste had a flashback of the enormous monarch butterfly. The words she had heard then echoed through her head. *I just want you to know what is possible.* Connor was trying to help her to believe that the impossible was actually possible.

"With time, you'll come to know and understand the truth," Star said confidently.

"So why is he around me?" Celeste asked. "Does he need something from me?

"He is around you because of love," Star replied. "It's what connects us. Love is the most powerful force in the universe."

"That seems like too simple of an explanation," Celeste protested. "There surely must be more to all of this than that."

"Of course. There is much more, but it all begins with love," Star continued. "He also wants you to know that he's okay and that he can hear you. He wants to protect you, guide you, and help teach you. More than anything, he wants to communicate with you, and he wants you to communicate back."

"But how can I do that?" Celeste asked.

"Well, you've already been communicating," Star said. "When you think of him and when you talk to him, he receives your messages. When you ask him questions, he tries to respond by sending you a sign, a song, or a message in a dream."

"That's not exactly what I had in mind," said Celeste. "I want to actually see him and be able to carry on a normal conversation with him. Is that possible?"

"Of course it is!" Star said. "I can teach you how to do exactly that."

"That's incredible!" exclaimed Celeste, her excitement and anticipation building.

"Yes, it truly is. Spirit communication is an amazing, precious gift. It allows us to stay in touch with those who have passed. They can still be a part of our lives, just in a different way. And if you want, you can learn to get a glimpse of their world, too. You can actually see and experience a tiny bit of heaven."

"How can I do that?" Celeste asked.

"I've developed a technique called 'the bridge of illumination.' I can help you get into a state of mind that enables you to cross a bridge and travel to Connor's world. You can meet him there and visit."

"For real?"

"Yes. You can actually be with Connor."

"Is it dangerous or harmful?" Celeste inquired.

"No, it's actually quite healthy and beneficial," Star said. "When you learn to do it the right way, you will notice your life becoming more peaceful and enriched. It's really quite healing and transformational."

"So, when can I get started?" Celeste asked eagerly.

"You can come by my office tomorrow, around one p.m.," Star offered.

"That sounds good," Celeste replied. "Thank you so much. I will see you then!"

Celeste hung up and danced around the house, elated. She would finally get to see Connor again! Oh, how she had missed him. She couldn't wait to connect with him.

CHAPTER 10
STAR LIGHT, STAR BRIGHT

Star Walker pulled her fiery hair back into a loose ponytail and sat down in her favorite brown leather chair to get ready for her meeting with Celeste. It was always important to mentally and emotionally prepare herself for spirit contact. She was looking forward to helping her new client better communicate with the spirit world and learn to visit there on her own.

First, she dimmed the lights and lit lavender candles throughout the room. Then she cleared her mind and engaged in a meditation. She took cleansing breaths, focused on the present moment, and tuned in to the energy all around her. Next, she said the Lord's Prayer and visualized her office surrounded in the powerful protection of a radiant, white light. This was to ensure no evil or malicious entities could get through. Opening herself and her clients up to the spirit world always required some protection. Although most spirits were kind and loving, a few hadn't yet received the healing and knowledge necessary to become beings of love and light. Their dark energy could interfere with connections and even, on rare occasions, make a person physically ill. Star wanted to make sure that any communication was from the highest source and always in the client's best interests. Her lifetime of experience and training had allowed her to perfect her technique, with which she always achieved the best possible results. She was proud and honored to have brought peace, comfort, and healing to thousands since first beginning her spirit work.

But it hadn't always been that way. As a young child, Star had been terrified of spirits. Many times she'd had trouble sleeping in her cozy bedroom, where her mother had created a peaceful environment for her. The walls were pale sky blue; the ceiling had fluffy clouds painted on it. Her delicate, white lace bedspread was accented with silky pillows in various shades of blue, some light and some dark. Several glow-in-the-dark stars and planets hung from the ceiling. Her mother knew that Star had trouble sleeping and was certain that this dreamy décor would help lull her precious daughter into a peaceful slumber. Unfortunately, it didn't.

Every night after dark, Star would see them clearly. They looked like ordinary men, women, and children, only they were surrounded by a translucent, white glow. Dozens of spirits gathered near her, mentally bombarding her with phrases, images, and messages. It was frightening and overwhelming for a small child. Star would do her best to tune them out, grabbing her fleece blanket in her tiny hands and tossing it over her head.

But although she couldn't see them under the security of her covers, she could always still hear them and feel them. The incessant buzzing of these many entities and the tingly electrical current running through her tiny body made it nearly impossible to sleep. She begged for them to leave her alone. But as the spirits told her time and time again, she was the one who could help them. This was her soul's purpose. They urged her to embrace her destiny and learn to harness the power within her and all around her. But what small child does that? Most don't even know what they want to eat for breakfast or what they want to be when they grow up. Giving a child such an enormous responsibility was indeed risky. Luckily God and the universe know exactly what they're doing and how to achieve optimal results. It was only a matter of time until Star understood her purpose and could utilize her talents. The first task was to get her well acquainted with the spirit world and help her to overcome her fears. The rest would come naturally as she got older and more mature.

So for many years, Star bravely faced the spirits each night, pushing her destiny aside so she could pretend to be a normal child. But she was always far from the typical kid. She had amazed her friends and relatives with her uncanny ability to know events before they even happened. It was always exciting when she predicted good events. Once, she approached her third grade teacher, Miss Marsh, and told her she was going to get married soon. Her teacher just chuckled and said, "Oh, Star, you're such a dreamer and an idealist. But I love your version of my life! If only it were true!"

Miss Marsh sighed and gazed off into the distance

with a hint of sadness in her eyes. Star didn't know it, but her teacher's boyfriend had recently broken up with her because he was afraid of commitment and didn't want to be tied down. So there were no wedding plans in Miss Marsh's future.

The next day her teacher arrived in the classroom with a huge, cheerful smile and a giant, pear-shaped diamond ring on her finger. She gave Star a big bear hug and said, "Star, you were so right! My ex-boyfriend came over last night and proposed! It was a complete surprise! I'm getting married in just a couple of months. Oh, honey, thank you for your sweet message of hope. You truly are a bright, shining star. I am a lucky teacher to have you in my class. Please, if you ever have any other messages for me, don't be afraid to tell me."

Star smiled a big, joyous grin. Her sapphire-blue eyes shone with love and excitement. She could feel her teacher's happiness, and it made her feel happy and special, too.

Star's gift, however, didn't just apply to good news. She also received many warnings and predictions of tragedies. These were always harder to accept, digest, and pass along. There were times when she kept her knowledge to herself for fear of frightening others. Other times, she believed that delivering the messages would help people to prepare for what lay ahead. It was always a tough call, but young Star did her best to evaluate her options and make the best possible decisions for the good of those involved.

Once, though, the decision got very personal. She was twelve years old. She fell asleep one Saturday afternoon, and images of the deceased danced around in her head. As usual, she clearly heard their many cries. They claimed that *it was time*. They said she was ready to fully embrace her gift and help both humankind and those who had passed. In her dream, Star expressed some doubts. She wasn't sure she was up for the challenge. She still wanted to be a child and have fun. She was afraid of the responsibility and didn't want to make a mistake that could mess up someone else's life.

"You won't," they assured her. "You will know what to do. Something big is coming, and it will change your life forever. It will lead you to your destiny. You are a healer, Star. And there will be much healing to do—both for yourself and for others."

Star didn't understand what this meant. What was coming? How would it change her life? She was suddenly filled with a sense of impending doom. Something really bad was about to happen.

Images flickered in her mind like pictures on a movie screen. She had a vision of her best friend, Chelsea, laughing and singing in the back seat of her father's car. The radio was blaring Donna Summer's "Last Dance." It was cloudy and raining, but the car was filled with exuberance. Chelsea was just like that—always brightening people's days with her enthusiasm and infectious smile.

Next Star saw a car weaving in and out of lanes as he headed toward the one that carried her best friend. The driver was depressed, careless, and distracted. In fact, he was suicidal and didn't care if he lived or died. She could feel his negative energy weighing down on her. She knew that nothing good could come of the situation. This man was a danger to both himself and others.

Star watched in horror as the vehicle sped up and traveled faster than she'd thought possible. In a moment of despair, the driver steered across the median and drove full-speed at a guardrail that protected those on the road from the waters below. He was going to end his life!

Unfortunately, his decision would take others with him. The intoxicated man didn't notice that another car was approaching when he made the choice to leave this world. That car, of course, was the one that carried Chelsea and her dad. Before anyone had time to think, the disturbed man's vehicle struck Chelsea's car. The impact was so strong that it broke the guardrail and sent both cars plummeting into the waters below. There was no way anyone could survive this. Star let out a piercing shriek of terror.

She awoke sweating, her heart pounding and filled with sadness and grief. She was about to lose her best friend: sweet, beautiful, spirited Chelsea. Should she tell anyone? Should she warn her friend and her dad? Star had learned at an early age that predicting anyone's death was a huge breach of trust. It crossed the line between being helpful and hurtful and could only result in the recipient's fear and anger. And that anger would be directed right at Star, the person who wanted nothing more than to help and heal others. As the spirits had told her from the time she was a tiny girl, her job was to heal and bring comfort, not interfere.

As much as she wanted to tell her friend everything, she could not divulge the details of this privileged information. As difficult as it was, she knew in her heart she wasn't supposed to stop the events that would soon take the life of her best friend and her father. Instead, she was meant to help their souls transition as they reached the other side. And she was meant to bring peace, comfort, and healing to those left behind. Was she really ready for this? She was only twelve years old, after all. Was she strong enough to bring peace and healing to others when she herself would be filled with overwhelming grief and sorrow?

Star knew she had no choice. She had to do what she had been chosen to do. She had been given her gifts for a reason, and now it was time to put them into practice. But first she needed to see Chelsea one last time. That certainly wasn't against the rules. Perhaps while she was there, she could even give her friend a gentle warning to be extra cautious. The rest was up to God and fate.

She got dressed quickly and raced over to Chelsea's house. Star didn't know how much time her friend had left, so she didn't want to waste a moment. When she knocked on the familiar door she had stood before so many times in the last eight years, she felt different. This time she wasn't there to chat about her day, discuss her latest crush, or trade outfits and jewelry with her friend: she was there to say good-bye.

Chelsea answered right away, and Star was relieved to see her. She gave her friend a long, tight hug. "Chelsea, I love you. You're the best friend I could ever ask for."

"Love you too, Star. What's up?" Chelsea asked, sensing her friend's sadness.

"Nothing's up. I just want you to know how much you mean to me. You do know I would do anything for you and that I'll always be there for you, no matter what, right?"

"Yes, I know that, Star." Chelsea smiled warmly. "Are you going somewhere?"

"No. I just had the urge to come over here."

"Okay, then. I need to get ready now. Dad and I are going to visit my grandmother in Las Vegas later. We're taking a road trip. You're psychic. Do you know if it's going to rain today?"

Star fought back tears and swallowed the lump that was now forming in her throat. "Yes, Chels. It's going to rain today. Please be extra careful on the roads today and take care of yourself."

"I will. I'll see you when I get back, BFF!"

Star would never forget that moment. She was confronted by the death of someone very dear to her, and all of her powers couldn't save Chelsea from her tragic fate.

After Chelsea's death, she was grief-stricken and desperate to find a way to set things right somehow. She couldn't just sit back and do nothing. This was too personal. She needed to find a way to resolve her own grief and bring comfort and closure to Chelsea's remaining family members. She came to realize just how important her abilities really were and finally accepted them.

From that moment on, she began experimenting with mediumship. She not only communicated with her friend after death, but opened herself up to help and heal others. She facilitated communication between Chelsea, her father and the family members left behind. She connected Chelsea's dad with his grieving wife. It was at this point that her abilities began to blossom. One by one the many spirits that had been visiting her since early childhood came with messages for their loved ones. Star carefully and lovingly delivered these messages, bringing peace and comfort to many. She even helped the tormented spirit of the man who had killed her friend, offering him forgiveness and directing him to the light, where he could heal his soul and become a guide for those still living. This man eventually chose to help those on earth who were struggling with alcoholism and severe depression. He would be their angel, nudging them along their path to recovery.

Star would be an earthly angel. Her intuition would offer valuable insight to those who needed it. And her ability to communicate with the dead would give the world hope and the chance to continue what they once believed were lost relationships.

Over the years Star became very good at what she did. She was no longer afraid of the many spirits that hovered around her and seemed to know exactly what to do to help them and their loved ones.

Now, thirty-five years after the tragedy that took her friend's life, she was a highly sought after and talented spirit communicator. She was considered an expert in her field. She was truly embracing her soul's purpose.

Star would never forget her first encounter with a newly deceased man named Connor. He had abruptly awakened her from a sound sleep several months ago; most spirits didn't have the energy to do that. This man's energy was much stronger than that of anyone she had ever encountered. When she opened her eyes and saw and felt him for the first time, she was astonished.

Connor had stood there at the foot of her bed, fully materialized. Although he appeared to be a man with wavy, brown hair and kind, brown eyes, he was definitely not of this world. He projected such a strong and loving energy unlike anything she had ever witnessed from a newly crossed soul. His strength and wisdom were so far advanced. He was a radiant being of love and light.

When he spoke about his true love, Celeste, his love intensified and filled the room with an overflow of emotion. Without ever having known this man, Star fell effortlessly in love with his energy and the divine presence that illuminated the room. It wasn't that she wanted him for herself. She simply was filled with the love and kindness that he projected. And she knew she would do anything to help him. He didn't need to convince her—or even ask. "What can I do for you?" she had asked eagerly.

"I need some help reaching Celeste. She is very sad about my death and is having trouble believing I'm okay. I haven't quite mastered the ability to appear in dreams, so I can't just tell her myself. Besides, if I did appear in a dream and told her I was fine, she would probably just conclude her mind made the dream up. She seems to have lost her faith in God and the afterlife these days. The message needs to be cryptic. Something that Celeste wouldn't initially understand, but would later find the answer to. Can you help me?"

"No problem. I can certainly do that for you. I travel into people's dreams delivering messages all the time. Any ideas on what sort of puzzle you want to use?"

"I'll leave the details to you. Just give her the name *Teisha*. I'm certain Celeste has never heard of the name before, and it means 'alive and well.' It will be the perfect way to get her thinking and wondering if there is more to this life than she realized."

"Ooh, I like it. Very clever, Connor. I'll be sure to visit Celeste tonight. I'll also help teach you how to enter her dreams when the time is right and she is ready to accept you. And maybe one day, I can even teach her how to cross the bridge of illumination and visit you in the spirit world."

"Thanks, Star. That would be great!" Connor said gratefully. "I look forward to that day."

Today was that day. It was the culmination of all of Celeste and Connor's experiences with each other. Star had been working with both of them for many months and couldn't wait to bring them together. She could already feel the love flowing and filling her office. The energy level was very high and absolutely incredible. Star had no doubt that today would eventually lead to great things. She knew from her visions that Celeste's soul purpose somehow involved Connor. She didn't have the details yet, but she was fully aware of the magnitude of their connection. And she was honored to be a part of it.

Her thoughts were interrupted by the ringing phone on her desk. "Star Walker," she answered.

"Ms. Walker, this is Sergeant Burns from the local police department. We have an urgent matter that we need some help with. Could you please meet us at one p.m.?"

So Star would have to reschedule her meeting with

Celeste. But she knew there were no accidents in the universe. This was happening for a reason. "Sure. What can I help you with, officer?"

"All I can tell you right now is that there is a local man we're investigating. We believe he's involved in several attempted rapes in the area. He may also be a suspect in another case. We want to see if you can pick up on anything with your abilities."

"No problem. I will see what I can do. I'll be down at the station at one."

"Thanks again, Ms. Walker."

"You're very welcome," she said kindly.

Star hung up and immediately dialed Celeste's cell phone. She had a feeling their meeting was just moments away.

CHAPTER 11
FIRST ATTEMPTS

*T*he next morning Celeste awoke at 4:44 a.m. She again wondered what was up with the repeating numbers. She was still seeing "1111" and "444" everywhere she went. It was time to get to the bottom of this! She decided she would look up what the numbers signified. She got out of bed and went to her mahogany desk a few feet away. Dave was still sleeping, so she tried to be extra quiet. She started up the computer and typed "repeating numbers" into the Google search box.

Celeste was amazed at how many results were listed that seemed to have something to do with numerology. She clicked on a link about seeing "1111." She read that noticing this number over and over tends to happen when one is about to go through a spiritual awakening. It is considered an "awakening code" that unlocks the subconscious mind and reminds us that we're spiritual

113

beings having a physical experience. Seeing "1111," the website explained, signals that someone is becoming more in tune with the spirit world and that unlikely and miraculous coincidences often accompany this. "Wow," thought Celeste. "That definitely fits with what's been going on lately."

She then looked up "444" and found that it meant that angels were with the person seeing it. Celeste immediately thought of Connor. He was certainly with her. But were there others? Was she being silently helped and guided by celestial beings?

She chuckled to herself when she thought of how strange her world had become. Not long ago she was just a successful, analytical accountant. And now she was about to visit a lady who claimed to talk to dead people and travel to the spirit world. *Am I insane?* Celeste wondered. Was it really possible to see and talk to Connor? Could she really somehow travel to his world? Everything just seemed so unbelievable and bizarre. But if it meant she could finally spend time with her lost love, she would give spirit communication a try.

Celeste showered quickly and got dressed in a comfortable blue blouse and black pants. She combed her shiny, golden hair and put on a coat of black mascara and dusty-rose lipstick.

When she got to the kitchen, she found Dave there drinking coffee. "Hello, beautiful," he said affectionately. "You look nice today."

"Thanks." She smiled.

"Where are you going on a Saturday morning?"

"I'm going to the office for a few hours to catch up on some work. Then I have an appointment."

"I didn't know you were going to the doctor today," he said with concern. "Are you okay?"

"It's not a doctor's appointment. It's a...*different* kind of appointment."

That hesitation. That look in her eyes. Dave had seen it many times before. Always when she was talking about Connor. "Does this have to do with Connor again?" he asked impatiently.

"Yes...well, maybe."

"Celeste, I thought you put all that behind you. I haven't heard you mention him lately."

"He sent me a rose."

"What? Connor? How could he send you a rose, Celeste? He's dead, remember?" Dave was getting worried now. He thought his wife had forgotten that Connor had died, or was hallucinating, or something. Was she losing touch with reality? Who was this rose really from?

"I know he's dead," Celeste said. "But he really did send me a rose." Celeste reached into her purse and pulled out the beautiful, delicate, pink fabric rose. She explained the whole story of how she had asked Connor for a sign and found the rose in the park.

Dave's jaw dropped, and he just stared at her in disbelief. He had always thought the whole spirit thing was outrageous. He had assumed that Celeste was imagining things because of her grief. But now he was starting to wonder if Connor really was reaching out to his wife from beyond the grave. He couldn't tell her that! If she thought for a minute that he might believe, it would drive her further away from him and closer to Connor. Dave didn't want that. The guy was dead, but he still had some kind of hold on her. He didn't want to share her love with any man—especially not a ghost. No, he had to keep quiet about this. He had to convince Celeste that the rose was just a coincidence.

"Oh, Celeste. I know you want to believe the rose was from Connor," he said soothingly. "But I'm certain it was nothing more than just a coincidence—an interesting one—but nonetheless, a meaningless, random event."

He still didn't believe her! Celeste was surprised. After telling her story, she was sure Dave would know that Connor was around her. Why didn't he believe her? Celeste was confident the rose had been a sign from Connor. It was just too perfect to be random. It all seemed like a carefully orchestrated event. Who finds a pink rose in a park underneath her seat? That certainly wasn't a common occurrence. And she knew it wasn't *meaningless*, like Dave suggested. She had actually asked Connor for a pink rose, just a week before she found it! "I'm not crazy," Celeste said firmly.

"I know, sweetheart. I never said you were. I only think your grief is causing you to assign meaning to something insignificant."

Celeste's heart sank. She couldn't believe that Dave thought the rose meant nothing. It was one of the most amazing gifts she had ever received from anyone. She knew it meant something. But she didn't want to stay and argue with him. She was eager to finish up some work and visit Star Walker. Star had been certain that Connor was around her quite often. She seemed to know this somehow. She was probably one of the few people who could help Celeste. Dave clearly wasn't willing or able to help her. He couldn't even accept that she was telling the truth.

"Well, I gotta go," she said, quickly brushing her lips on his cheek. "Give Chip a hug and kiss for me when he wakes up. I'll be home around three."

"Okay, honey. See you later. But, wait—you didn't tell me about this appointment," Dave said nervously.

"It's no big deal, really," Celeste replied, trying to downplay her meeting. "I'm just seeing this lady who may be able to help me sort things out."

"Oh," Dave said, his heart sinking. "Well, just remember that *I'm* your husband, and I love you very much. And you certainly can't have any sort of a relationship with a dead guy. Don't lose sight of what's most important."

Celeste was a bit surprised by his response. Dave actually sounded concerned. He still felt threatened by Connor! He was jealous. She got the impression that he was afraid of losing her. "Don't worry, hon," Celeste said reassuringly. "It will be fine."

Dave, however, was *very* worried. He tried not to show it, but he now secretly feared that Celeste might actually be able to have a relationship with a ghost. *He's sending her roses! It sure seems to me like he's trying to win her over. I never thought I would have to compete with a spirit*, Dave thought angrily. *But the question is, what can I do about it?* Celeste, who had no idea what was going through Dave's mind, smiled politely and gave him another quick peck on the cheek.

She eagerly headed out to her blue Ford Fusion, optimistic about what the future would bring. Starting the engine, she grabbed her sunglasses off the console and turned on the radio. Pink Floyd's "Hey You" was playing.

"Hey you, yourself." She giggled. She got the feeling Connor was just as eager to talk as she was. She wished she didn't have to work this morning. She would much rather not wait until afternoon. Just as she thought that, her cell phone rang. "Hello?"

"Celeste, it's Star Walker. Something's come up, and I can't meet with you at one. I'm so sorry. I do have some time this morning, if you want to come by earlier."

"How about right now?"

"Perfect. I'll see you soon."

Celeste was ecstatic that she would be able to talk to Connor soon. Or so she hoped. She was restless and had no idea how she would get any work done today, anyway. This change of times was just what she needed. Was this a coincidence? Or was it some perfectly orchestrated event arranged by Connor, the angels, or God? She'd never know for sure, but she did know for certain that the timing was absolutely perfect!

The sunlight flickered through the trees as Celeste drove to Star's. She was filled with hope and anticipation. She thought about what she wanted to say to Connor. She wanted him to know that she had always loved him—even when she let him go. She had never stopped loving him. She wanted him to know how much she regretted not being a part of his life before he died. She especially longed to hug him. She also just had to find out what he was doing around her and why.

As Celeste pulled into the parking lot at Star's office, Pink Floyd began playing once again. This time, it was "Comfortably Numb."

"Hello, Connor," Celeste said. "I can hear you. And after today, maybe I will be able to see you, too." She parked and headed in. She had no idea what awaited her, but she knew it would be good.

Star Walker looked exactly like she had in Celeste's dreams—the same reddish-orange hair and kind, sparkling, sapphire-blue eyes. She even wore the same outfit, a blue and cream calico blouse and tan pants. Celeste felt like she was visiting with an old friend instead of seeing a psychic medium for the first time. They didn't have to get acquainted before getting down to business. They already seemed to have a good rapport. It must have been because they had met before in Celeste's dreams.

"Well, let's start at the beginning. What questions do you have about spirit communication?" Star asked.

"My biggest question is: how is it possible? If the dead are in heaven, and we are on earth, how can they travel to us, and how can we travel to them?"

"Good questions. First of all, heaven isn't way up in the sky, like many people believe. It's actually all around us. The reason we can't see it is because we live in a different dimension. Have you ever heard of parallel worlds?"

"Yes, that's when two worlds exist simultaneously in the same space. But isn't that fiction?" Celeste asked.

"It's actually a fact." Star smiled. "There are many dimensions to reality. Many worlds exist right here, right now. But most of the time, we're only tuned in to the world we live in—the physical plane. Think of the spirit world as an invisible overlay to our world. It's always here. Our loved ones in spirit are always close by. But we often fail to see or hear them, because we're not tuned in to them and their world."

"Kind of like adjusting the dial on a radio or television, huh?" Celeste asked, seeming to understand.

"Exactly."

"But that doesn't explain how we can communicate with each other," Celeste said. "How can we tune in to their station?"

"That's all about frequency. Everything in the universe vibrates. Some things vibrate at the same frequencies; others vibrate at different frequencies. When two objects vibrate at the same frequency—and one affects the other—you get something called 'harmonic resonance.' You hear a lot about resonance and its application to music, physics, and electronics. What many people don't realize is that the exact same principle applies to people and the spirit world."

Celeste listened intently as Star described the fundamentals of how the universe operates. She was fascinated and intrigued. A whole new world was opening up to her, testing her former beliefs and transforming her very existence.

"Everything in the universe is made up of energy," Star continued. "People are energy. Thoughts are energy. Everything we say, do, feel, or think sends out energy into the atmosphere. That energy is then transferred to another object, person, or being. For example, if you are angry or sad, people around you can subconsciously feel your emotions. They absorb some of that energy and often wind up feeling sad or angry also. They may not always understand why, but they do recognize a shift in their moods and feelings. In simple terms, we *affect* each other.

"Similarly, when you have a thought or feeling

about someone who passed, they actually receive your energy—no matter where they are. They can hear your thoughts and feel your pain, your sadness, and your love for them. If you are on the same wavelength as the person you are thinking of, then the two of you can actually communicate telepathically, back and forth. Sometimes this happens in a dream; other times, you will receive words, phrases, and images in your mind. You may also notice meaningful coincidences, otherwise known as synchronicity. You can ask the person in spirit questions or request specific signs, and they will do their best to answer you."

"I've done this," exclaimed Celeste excitedly. "I've asked Connor for signs, and I've always gotten exactly what I asked for!"

"Yes, you have," said Star. "That is the simplest form of after-death communication. Many people ask their loved ones in spirit for signs, but not everyone receives them. As I've said, it's all about frequency. Some people become disappointed when they ask a deceased friend or relative for a sign and nothing happens. They wonder why others have gotten signs, and they haven't."

"So, how do you explain that?" Celeste asked curiously.

"I mentioned earlier that in order to communicate with the deceased, you have to be on their frequency. You need to tune in to them. This isn't always easy, and some people cannot achieve this. No matter how hard they try, they can't seem to match the frequency of the spirit they are trying to connect with. This doesn't mean that the spirit can't hear them. It just means that two-way communication isn't possible."

"Please tell me more," said Celeste. "What about those who *are* able to have two-way communication? How exactly does that work?"

"When two souls vibrate at the same frequency, that creates harmonic resonance between them," Star explained. "Harmonic resonance is what makes spirit communication possible. It's like being in perfect rhythm with another being." She clarified: "First, picture a sine wave. It's very regular, with each hill and valley flowing seamlessly into the next. Now, think of the waves of an ocean and how they flow rhythmically back and forth, in perfect timing. Picture a child swinging on a swing, back and forth. Or imagine the leaves on a tree gently swaying from side to side. All of these things have a certain pattern and natural rhythm and flow to them. There is a consistent, systematic order to all of them. Now, think of all the bricks arranged to form a wall. We are like those bricks. We are all parts of a whole. Every living being is connected together to make up the entire universe. We are all one entity. This oneness is harmonic resonance at its best."

Celeste found the description fascinating. She thought she and Connor must be on the same wavelength already, and that it was why he could send her messages. They were somehow tuned in to each other's frequencies. Why then couldn't she physically see him?

"You can't see Connor because you are too distracted by the physical world," Star answered, reading her mind. "Every day, everywhere we go, we are bombarded by so much stimuli—traffic, horns honking, people coming and going, music playing, children laughing, dogs barking, animals scurrying about, refrigerators humming, birds chirping, lights turning on and off. You get the idea. We need to train your mind to enter a relaxed, receptive state. You need to be in a place where the distractions of the physical world fade into the background. Then you will be able to cross the bridge of illumination and meet with Connor."

Celeste wanted to know more about the bridge of illumination. Star explained that it was an image that one's mind can conjure up while in deep hypnosis. When people get really good at seeing the bridge in their minds, they can then open their eyes and actually see the bridge manifesting in the physical world. At this point, crossing the bridge becomes real and tangible, just like walking across the street.

"It's like the portal or gateway to heaven," Star said. "Once you cross it, you're actually in another dimension—the spirit world."

"Amazing!" Celeste beamed. "Let's get started."

To begin, Star told Celeste, she would guide her through some relaxation exercises. Celeste would progressively and intentionally relax each muscle in her body. She would clear her mind and just let go. Once she was in a totally relaxed state, Star would then ask her to practice creative visualization: the art of visualizing certain images in the mind. After that, Celeste would just lie there quietly and see what images appeared on their own. These scenes would be actual glimpses of the spirit world, otherwise known as "echoes of paradise." She would be able to see Connor there and receive any messages he had for her. With more practice, she would be able to actually touch him, feel him, and carry on a conversation.

Celeste felt a wave of excitement run through her body from head to toe. She wanted so much to touch Connor again. She hoped with all her heart that it would be possible.

The relaxation exercises went well. Celeste found herself more relaxed than she had been in years. Star asked her to picture a beautiful flower in her mind. Celeste immediately saw an image of a pink rose, just like the one Connor had left for her in the park. Star then had her imagine herself spinning around in a field of yellow and purple wildflowers, feeling happy and free. Without any trouble, Celeste could picture herself there. After a few more images, Celeste was ready to see what came to her. She was ready to take a glimpse into the spirit world.

At first Celeste saw total darkness. She took a slow, cleansing breath. She could feel herself slipping deeper and deeper into a tranquil state. Fears dissipated. Tension melted away like cotton candy on her tongue. She totally cleared her mind and waited to see what came to her.

Celeste began to visualize a beach scene. She could see the beige sand, blue waves, and seagulls. She could feel the warm, gentle breeze caressing her skin. It was a beautiful, serene place. As Celeste looked around admiring the scenery, she saw the figure of a man walking in the distance. He slowly and confidently wandered toward her. It was Connor! As he approached her, she noticed that he looked happy and peaceful. He wore a white cotton shirt and blue jeans that comfortably adorned his body. He looked heavenly, angelic even.

And he was smiling at her! He handed her a single yellow rose.

Yellow? What happened to the pink rose, like I got in the park? Celeste thought. She was really surprised by the yellow one. After she thought that, Connor then gave her pink roses, too.

That scene faded, and Celeste then saw her grandmother on her dad's side. Grandma Moore had passed away four years ago. She looked young and happy and was smiling at Celeste. She splashed in the waves, wearing a two-piece, green-and-white-checkered bathing suit. Her shoulder-length, silvery-blonde hair glistened in the sunlight.

Her grandma faded from view, and then Connor came back again. He gave Celeste a yellow rose, then a pink rose, followed by a red rose and a white rose. Then he flashed her a big smile and started laughing. He thought it would be funny to give her one of each color, since she had questioned the yellow rose earlier. Connor always did have a good sense of humor!

Celeste felt her eyes fill with tears. She was overwhelmed by the intensity of the experience. There was so much love and happiness here that her body just couldn't stay in that state for very long. Connor faded, and she opened her eyes, disappointed.

"Celeste, that was awesome!" Star said excitedly.

"But I couldn't stay," Celeste said sadly. "Connor disappeared."

"That's okay. For most people, it takes three or four tries before they can connect to the spirit world at all. Some never can connect. You nailed it on your first try!"

"Does this mean I'll be able to do better next time?"

"Most definitely!" Star said reassuringly. "How about if I see you in a few days? Just call when you're ready to try again."

Celeste agreed and grabbed her purse and coat. She gave Star a big hug and thanked her for the help. As she got into her car and turned on the radio, Pink Floyd's "Wish You Were Here" was playing again. A huge smile crept across her face.

"I wish I was there too, Connor!" she said. "But don't you worry. I will definitely be visiting you very soon."

Celeste felt a soft, soothing tickle brush her right cheek. It felt sort of like lips on her skin. *Did he just kiss me?* she wondered. Celeste grinned from ear to ear all the way home, just like after the first time he had kissed her many years ago.

CHAPTER 12
RUDE AWAKENING

*T*he ringing phone at Celeste's bedside jolted her out of a sound sleep. She glanced at the clock. It was 4:44 a.m. Who could be calling her this early? Was something wrong? With her heart beating rapidly in her chest, she breathlessly answered the phone. "Hello," she croaked.

"Celeste?"

"Sue? What's wrong, sweetie?"

"Sorry to call so early, but I thought you should know. Andy just called me."

"Andy? What did that jerk want?" Celeste had flashbacks of her abusive ex-boyfriend hitting her and then telling her he was sorry and that he loved her. Yeah, right. That was sure a display of affection! Why would he call Sue so early in the morning?

"Andy said that you belong to him," Sue said with

127

alarm in her voice. "He said he never should have let you get away. He talked all about Connor and how he stole you from him. Then he mentioned Dave. He said Dave paid him off to stay away from you."

"Figures," Celeste said, thinking of how Dave had always been jealous of any contact she had with other men and thought money could buy love. "Was he stoned?"

"I don't think so. He was crying and talking about how you were the only one who ever really understood him. You were the only one who was kind to him."

"Yeah, I understood him, all right," Celeste said bitterly. "He was an abusive asshole!"

"There's more," said Sue. "He said he was coming to rescue you from the pompous rich dude, and that he knew what you needed to be happy. I thought I should warn you. He sounded very agitated. I'm afraid he might try to come to your house."

Just as Sue said that, Celeste heard a screech of tires outside her window. "Oh, shit!" she blurted. "I think he's already here. I gotta go."

Celeste peered out the window and watched as Andy headed around the back of her house. *Oh crap,* she thought, *Chip's window is open. Andy might try to come in that way. What if he hurts Chip? Or worse yet, what if he kidnaps him?*

Her heart pounding, Celeste grabbed her robe and headed out the front door. She had to protect her child, no matter what the cost. And she had to act quickly. She had no choice but to face Andy alone.

She reached the back patio just as Andy was approaching Chip's window.

"Celeste, baby!" Andy cried, flinging his arms around her.

"What are you doing here, Andy?" she asked sharply.

"What do you mean? I belong here. We belong together, remember?"

"No, Andy, we don't."

"How can you say that?" he said. "After all we've been through. You are so special to me. Don't you know that by now? I love you, baby!"

"Hitting a woman and insulting her all the time is not love, Andy. It's called abuse."

"I know. I'm sorry. I never meant to hurt you. I want to make it up to you," he said sweetly. "I know what you want. I know how to love you properly. Let me show you."

Celeste cringed as he grabbed her fiercely and pulled her against him. She knew he was determined to make her his again. He kissed her violently, his lips stinging against her skin. He tugged on the back of her hair and then pushed her forcefully to the ground.

A wave of terror came over Celeste, and she let out a shriek. She knew what he was about to do. This is what Andy always did when he wanted sex. He didn't ask. He didn't romance her. He just took. Andy held down Celeste's arms with one hand and untied her robe, exposing her breasts. A sharp stabbing sensation pierced through her as he sank his teeth into her flesh. Her breast throbbed as she tried with all her might to push him off. But he was too strong.

Celeste felt like a helpless child, lying there in the grass outside of her house. All the fear, the shame, and the humiliation she had once felt with him came rushing back to her. "Andy, please. No!" she cried. "This isn't how you love someone."

"Sure, it is. That's why they call it making love. Don't you know anything, you stupid bitch?"

"I know all about love, and this isn't it! Please don't do this," she pleaded. "If you really, truly love me, you won't."

"Oh, I love you, all right," he said confidently. "And when I'm done, you'll know exactly how much." He unzipped his pants.

Celeste jumped up quickly and tried to get away, but Andy was too quick. In a flash his pants were off and he grabbed her, pushing her to the ground again. He tore off her underwear and climbed on top of her, ready to make her his again.

Just as he was about to rape her, there was a huge gust of wind and a bright flash of light. Andy stopped abruptly. A crash of thunder echoed through the early morning sky, and rain started to pour. Andy heard a strange hum and noticed that the window on his new, shiny, red Corvette was rolling down on its own. Rain poured in. "What the hell?" he said, startled. Then the convertible top also retracted, and the rain shower intensified. "My leather seats will be ruined!" he yelled as he raced for the car.

Celeste slowly rose from the spot where she had been trapped. She grabbed her robe and put it on as she watched Andy fight with his car and try to get the top back up. It was then that she saw it: a hazy cloud of glowing, blue light, directly above Andy's car. How odd! What was that? Then she clearly heard Connor's voice coming from the direction of the mysterious light. "Run, Celeste! Get inside the house and lock the door. Hurry up!"

She bolted into the house while Andy was oblivious. He was still struggling with his car, baffled by the strange malfunction. But Celeste now knew the source of the disruption. It wasn't Mother Nature, and it wasn't just a lucky rainstorm. Connor had saved her from Andy once again. Just like old times. He really was her guardian angel. Now more than ever, she was thankful for his ethereal presence in her life.

CHAPTER 13
ON THE OTHER SIDE

"*I* think you should press charges," Dave said sternly later that morning. "That man assaulted you and tried to rape you."

"No," Celeste said. "That will just make him angrier and more violent. I know Andy. I don't want to stir him up more. He doesn't need jail time; he needs professional help."

"You're sweet, Celeste," said Dave. "But I really think he belongs in jail."

"Trust me on this, Dave. The madder he gets, the more violent he becomes," Celeste explained. "I don't want to piss him off more. Even if he were sent to jail, he would be so mad when he got out. I'd be afraid he'd try to come after you or Chip. I need my family to be safe. This is better left alone."

"Okay, but are you sure you're all right?" he asked

with concern. "You seem shaken."

"I'm fine," Celeste lied. She felt edgy and distressed. Who knows how badly Andy would have hurt her if Connor hadn't showed up. Thank God for Connor! He was really looking out for her. She hadn't told Dave yet about that part, because she knew he was already concerned about her feelings for Connor. If Dave knew he had saved her, he would probably really freak out. What husband wants to hear that while he was sleeping soundly, his wife's ex-boyfriend was the one protecting her? That would just make him feel so inferior. She didn't want to do that to Dave. She didn't want him to know just how much a part of her life Connor had become.

Celeste knew she had to see Connor again soon. She needed to thank him. She wanted to spend time with him in that wonderful, peaceful, mesmerizing place. She needed to find out more about spirit communication and the afterlife. But she also had a life here. As hard as it was, she decided that she needed to tell Dave what had really happened earlier that morning. Their relationship might be rocky, but he was still her husband. "Dave, I need to tell you something important," Celeste said with hesitation.

"What is it, babe?" Dave asked, obviously concerned.

"It's about last night."

"Andy did hurt you, didn't he? That bastard!"

"No. Really, I'm fine. But I wouldn't have been if it wasn't for..." Celeste sat there at the kitchen table, her words frozen in her mouth. She wanted to explain how Connor had mysteriously appeared at just the right moment, but she wasn't sure how Dave would react. Would he think she was crazy or imagining things again? Would he be angry? Would he feel jealous or threatened? She just didn't know.

"Celeste, honey, it's okay. You can tell me anything," Dave said, gently stroking her golden hair. "Please, confide in me. You can trust me."

Celeste swallowed. "Well…last night, when Andy attacked me…something—someone—helped me!"

"What do you mean?" asked Dave, wondering if a passerby had intervened. Celeste explained the scenario and how she had witnessed the hazy, blue cloud and clearly heard Connor's voice. She talked quickly and nervously, unsure what to expect from Dave. When she finished, she looked at her husband and found tears rolling down his cheeks. In all of their married life, she had only seen him cry once—when his mother had passed away.

"Dave, honey, I'm sorry. Have I upset you?"

"No, you didn't do anything," he said softly. "I just feel like I've lost you."

"I'm still here."

"Physically, yes. But your heart belongs to him. Your heart has always belonged to him. I guess I knew that all along, but I figured since you married me and he lived so far away, that everything would be okay. Then, after you told me he died, I was certain he was no longer a threat to our relationship. Now I see the truth: nothing can ever separate you from Connor. Not time, not space. Not even death."

"Oh, Dave," Celeste said sympathetically, giving him a hug.

"I'm sorry, Celeste. I can't compete with him anymore. I can't save your life by causing a rainstorm. I can't make a rose materialize in the park. I see the way your face lights up when you talk about him. It's the same way it lit up when you first told me about him in college. A love like that just never dies."

"So, what are you saying, Dave?"

"I'm saying that I love you, and I really want us to stay together. But I fear you're already gone."

"No, honey, I'm not," Celeste said firmly. "Connor may be a part of my life somehow, but he's not the father of my child. He can't be my husband. He can't give me a hug or a home or take me out to dinner. He can't make love to me. I need you."

"So, you're not going to leave me?"

"No, Dave. I'm not going anywhere. As long as you're okay with Connor hanging around sometimes."

"Well, I'll admit, it's kind of weird. And I do feel jealous. I don't want to lose you to a ghost. I feel like he's taking you away from me sometimes. But I guess it wouldn't hurt to have a guardian angel around once in a while. He did save you from Andy, after all. I'm so thankful to him for that."

"Well, then. Let's get ready for breakfast. Chip will be up soon." Dave, feeling relieved, gave Celeste a long, passionate kiss. As he kissed her, she imagined she was kissing Connor. "I love you, Connor," she said.

"What did you just say?" Dave asked angrily.

"I love you...Dave," Celeste replied, slowing as she realized her mistake.

"I can't do this!" Dave yelled. "I can't be with you if your heart is with him!" He headed out the front door and slammed it behind him.

Celeste didn't know if he was coming back or not. Maybe they really were through this time. She really couldn't blame him. Dave was right. Even though she was married to him, her heart and soul clearly belonged to someone else.

✽ ✽ ✽

A few days later, Celeste sat silently in her office, deep in thought. The humid air and blazing summer sun penetrated her window and left her feeling hot and uncomfortable. She was also uncomfortable with how unpredictable and unfamiliar her life had become. She still hadn't heard from Dave. She left messages on his cell phone, but he wasn't returning any of her calls. She knew he was fine, because he had called her mother's house and talked to Chip several times. He had also stopped by there and had lunch with their son while Celeste was at work. But he hadn't spoken to her since she had called him by Connor's name the other night.

Celeste was upset with herself and truly felt sorry for her husband. She had never wanted to hurt him. She wasn't intentionally trying to ruin their relationship. But she couldn't help where her heart was leading her. It wasn't her choice; it was just the way she felt. Maybe someday he would come around and forgive her. She hoped so, since they had been trying so hard to keep their family together. It wasn't good for Chip to see them at odds. He needed two loving parents. He needed stability and an example of what true love really was. Unfortunately, they were unable to give that to him.

Celeste's boss interrupted her thoughts. "Are you getting ready to leave?"

"Yeah, I have an appointment soon, and then I'm heading home," she replied.

"Okay. Please get some rest. You look tired. Has Dave called yet?"

"No."

For a brief moment, Celeste thought she saw Jeremy's face light up. Could this scrawny little man, who had been her boss since she graduated from college, have romantic feelings for her? Did he think he might have a chance? She found that surprising and a tad funny. Then he turned serious. "Really, Celeste," he said. "I worry about you...as a friend. I don't want you to be upset or unhappy. You're a wonderful person, and you deserve the best."

"Thanks, Jer," she said kindly. "Don't worry about me. I'll be fine. See you tomorrow."

Celeste left work and headed over to Star's office to attempt another connection with Connor. She needed to see him more than ever now. Andy had almost raped her. Her husband had walked out on her. Her life was falling apart. She never felt that way when she was with Connor. Somehow when she was with him, her life magically came together.

As Celeste and Star got ready to begin their session, Star had an excited look on her face. "I have a really good feeling about this," she explained hopefully, her blue eyes twinkling like sapphires. "I detect a strong energetic balance all around. I feel that you and Connor have become even more in tune lately. Did something big happen recently? I feel like there was some sort of struggle and danger. He rescued you, for some reason."

"He did," Celeste said gratefully. "At least, I think it was him. Someone, or something, saved me from being raped a few days ago. I saw a blue light and thought I heard his voice."

"Oh, honey! How terrible that you were almost raped!" Star exclaimed. "That must be the danger and struggle I felt. This man who tried to hurt you is very troubled. It's a good thing Connor was there for you."

"He seemed to know just when to show up," Celeste said.

"Your energies are becoming stronger and more complementary," Star said enthusiastically. "His act of love and kindness has made him more connected to you. This is a great step toward stronger and more frequent harmonic resonance. Let's give the connection a try and see what we get."

Star led Celeste through the initial procedure, and Celeste found herself slipping off into a dreamlike state right away. First she saw a glorious field of purple and yellow wildflowers. She spun around and around in the field with her arms outstretched. She could feel the breeze blowing her hair back and whipping it about. She felt so peaceful and free, like a bird soaring through the sky. Soon she spotted a majestic, glowing bridge. It reminded her of the Golden Gate Bridge in San Francisco, only it was surrounded by colorful lights, like Niagara Falls at night. It was the bridge of illumination, the gateway to the afterlife. "Do you see it?" Star asked.

"Yes," Celeste said softly. "It's absolutely stunning, and so beautiful."

"Focus on it. Picture it appearing in the physical

world. Know that you can cross it and visit Connor. Believe you have the power to be with him." She paused for a few minutes to allow Celeste time to ready herself for the journey to the other world. Celeste was preparing to cross the threshold into heaven, a journey that must always be approached with the utmost love, patience, and care. "Now, slowly open your eyes, and tell me if you still see it."

Celeste did as Star told her. The bridge was still there! At the end of Star's office, the side of the building had opened up to reveal the magnificent bridge. It was right there in front of her, beckoning her to proceed. She approached it with awe and wonder, looking up and admiring its beauty. Then she took a cleansing breath and walked slowly and cautiously across.

Connor stood there, waiting for her on the other side. He was smiling and had a white glow all around him. They embraced as if they hadn't seen each other in years, each clinging to the other like they never wanted to let go. The white glow enveloped both of them, creating a whirlwind of love.

Connor then took Celeste's hand and led her to a white stone park bench with a bright pink rhododendron next to it. They sat down, and she asked him why he was really here with her. He said he was making up for lost time.

Then he led her to a beautiful rose garden filled with different-colored rosebushes. Butterflies flew all around them—little yellow and white ones, and a few small monarchs. She heard birds happily chirping melodic songs. It was an amazing place filled with peace, love, and forgiveness. She needed all of those things in her life right now. "I'm sorry for not staying in touch with you," Celeste said sweetly.

"It's okay. You're in touch now," Connor replied.

"But you're dead."

"It's never too late."

"So, will you be my spirit friend?" Celeste asked, hoping she and Connor could stay connected in some way.

"I already am." He smiled.

"Why are you around me so much?"

"Because I never stopped caring about you," he said sincerely. "And because you're one of the few people who's able to communicate with me."

Celeste then asked Connor if all of the strange happenings in her life were things he had done. Had he lain down behind her in bed that night? Had he been responsible for all the songs? Was he really the one who had saved her from Andy?

He admitted to all of those incidents, and more. He told her he had been around her quite often and had been trying really hard to reach her in any way he could. Connor also expressed a strong desire to protect her and help guide her in life.

He then took a gold, heart-shaped box out of his pocket and handed it to Celeste. She opened it and found a gorgeous necklace with two hearts joined together by a tiny pink rose. It reminded her of the pink rose she had found in the park and seemed symbolic of her spiritual journey. Connor gently put the necklace around her neck. He said it would be a reminder of him and to always believe. "Thanks for saving me from Andy," Celeste said gratefully.

"No problem," he replied. "There is no way I could let him do that to you."

"It's so good to see you," Celeste said as she reached up and gently stroked his face. She could actually feel his smooth, warm skin!

"It's good to see you, too." He smiled, giving her a soft kiss on the forehead. Celeste asked him how he was doing and if he had any other messages or advice for her. He said he was doing fine and felt happy and peaceful.

He then reminded her of the giant monarch butterfly that had been right in her path. She saw a flashback of the butterfly gently and slowly opening and closing its wings as if to say hello and recalled how it had flown so high into the sky as she watched it disappear into the clouds. She remembered being amazed at its incredible height; she had never witnessed anything like it before.

Connor confirmed that he had shown her that butterfly so she would know what was possible. He wanted her to experience the wonder and magic of the universe. She needed to know that there was so much more to life than she had ever realized. Now he had something else to show her.

Celeste then saw a beautiful, crystal-clear lake surrounded by pine trees. A small boat was docked at the shore. Not far from the lake was a sparkling stream and a cascading waterfall. He then showed her a forest with very tall trees and sunlight peeking in through the rich, green leaves.

They went for a walk through the woods. Celeste enjoyed the gorgeous scenery and the comfort of Connor's company. Her mind was clear, so she was able to take in all that was around her and truly appreciate it.

As they walked hand in hand through the dense forest, she spotted a hawk circling above them. Celeste admired its strength, captivated by the way the bird coasted through the sky effortlessly.

Connor and Celeste soon emerged from the forest into the bright light once again. Celeste was astonished to see a mosaic pattern with a rainbow of bright colors just above her. The colors were very vivid and vibrant. It was like she was dreaming, only she was fully conscious. She had entered a magical world where few venture—a place where life and death meet in a mingling of sight, feelings, and sensations. It was a special, sacred place, far beyond her wildest dreams. And Connor was there! She was with him. Somehow he was showing her things and talking to her as if he were physically present. Could this be real? Had she really entered his world? Or was this all just a dream or a figment of her imagination? Celeste was determined to make sense of it all. She was driven to find the truth about everything. "It's real, Celeste," said Connor, reading her mind. "Don't stop believing. Please don't doubt your feelings. You are actually here with me. Welcome to heaven."

"It's beautiful beyond belief," Celeste said in astonishment.

"Please come back and visit me again," he said. "There is so much I want to share with you, so much I want to teach you." Then he kissed her softly and slowly faded from her sight.

Celeste was left standing there in this incredible paradise, totally in awe and surrounded by unimaginable beauty. For the first time in a long time, she didn't feel alone. She was no longer sad or helpless. Instead, she was left with a sense of love, hope, peace, and encouragement.

Maybe the bridge between this life and the next wasn't so difficult to cross, after all. Celeste looked forward to learning more and attempting to enter a world once unknown and inaccessible to her. This was just the beginning of her remarkable journey.

CHAPTER 14
BOAT TRIP

*J*ust a few short days after Celeste's miraculous visit to Connor's world, she craved more. She wanted to experience the beauty and magic of heaven. She ached to be with Connor again.

It was a great time to try to visit him again, since Chip was spending the night with his grandmother. She still hadn't heard from Dave. It had been about a week now since he had stormed off. It was just after 7:00 p.m.; the house was quiet and lonely, and she had all night to herself. Celeste honestly couldn't think of anything she would rather do than spend some time with Connor.

She went into the living room and found a comfortable spot on the cushiony, tan sofa. She closed her eyes, said a prayer, and began the muscle relaxation exercises that Star Walker had taught her. When she opened her eyes, she saw the bridge of illumination more clearly than before. Tiny flecks of rainbow colors reflected off of it. She took a deep breath and effortlessly glided across the bridge.

Connor greeted her with a smile and a hug. He seemed eager to share what Celeste had missed in his life after they had parted on earth.

He led her to his small boat, took her hand, and helped her climb aboard. They went out on the lake, and he flashed her a big smile. He stopped the boat in the middle of the lake. Quietness and peacefulness surrounded them. He took out a fishing rod, put a worm on it, and began fishing.

The word "bluegill" came to Celeste's mind, and she saw an image of a fish. Connor showed her how to fish, and she tried it. She did pretty well and actually caught a few. They stayed for a while, enjoying the stillness and quietness. Celeste felt serene and blissful.

After the boat trip, Connor took Celeste to his house. It was a tan cape cod with green shutters and a huge front porch. There was a warm, gentle breeze that soothed their souls and renewed their spirits. On the front porch, they sat down on a white park bench. As she looked around, Celeste breathed in the fresh air that smelled of pine. Lots of tall, green trees bordered the yard. It was a tranquil, beautiful site. They sat there for quite some time, relaxing and quietly enjoying the peacefulness. There was nowhere else Celeste would rather be. "So, do you have any advice on how to live my life?" she asked.

"Well, it would help if you could learn to let go, believe, and not be so afraid of things," he replied.

"Okay, that's fair. What else?"

"Embrace and enjoy life. Appreciate the beauty that

is all around you."

"Like we're doing right now."

"Exactly." He smirked. Celeste thought about how much she had learned and experienced since Connor's passing. Her whole world, her outlook on life, and her beliefs had been forever changed. She now knew for certain that life continues after death. She also knew that those who die can communicate with their loved ones left behind. And, she better understood the limitless power of love. But with all that she had discovered, she still wanted and needed more. She felt as if her learning and spiritual development were just beginning. There was so much more she wanted to know.

"Will you continue to help me and guide me?" she asked Connor.

"Yes, when I can."

"Thanks, Connor." She smiled.

They sat for what felt like hours, quietly enjoying the serenity and stillness of their tranquil surroundings. Somehow when she was with him in this glorious place, time stood still. Yesterday and tomorrow didn't exist— only here and now. It felt good to let go of time and space. It was freeing, liberating, exhilarating. She felt lighter and unencumbered by the physical and emotional baggage that weighed her down on earth. Still, she was human, with human needs and emotions. She was in Connor's world, but she didn't yet belong here. There always came a time when her mind and her body signaled that she needed to return to the physical world.

"I'm getting tired now, so I better go," she said softly, disappointed that the time had come to leave once again. They hugged like old friends, and Connor kissed her right cheek.

Celeste rose from her seat and headed back to the spot where the bridge of illumination was waiting for her. When she came back across it and opened her eyes, Dave was in the living room, just staring at her. Startled, she jumped. "How long have you been standing there?" she asked, concerned that he had witnessed her crossing the bridge from the spirit world. She feared he would be upset or angry with her for visiting Connor.

"Just a few minutes. I think I was having an ocular migraine," he answered. "I saw some weird, colored lights, and it looked like a spot on our wall had opened up. I closed my eyes for a few minutes, and when I opened them, you suddenly appeared, right in the middle of the colored lights. I thought maybe you went for an evening walk, because I didn't see you anywhere in the house. Wow, Celeste! I've never seen you look so glowing and radiant. It makes me fall in love with you all over again."

"Oh, Dave. That's so sweet." She blushed. "Do you still see the bizarre images?"

"No. All I see is you, looking more beautiful than ever. You're mesmerizing!" He planted a warm, moist kiss on her lips. Then he reached behind his back and pulled out a bouquet of colorful wildflowers. "I'm so sorry for last week," he said sweetly. "I shouldn't have stormed off like that. I was so angry with you...and him. I just needed some time to think."

"It's okay." Celeste smiled. "It was my fault. You had every right to be angry."

"I'm trying hard to understand, but it isn't easy for

me, you know?"

"I know. I'm sorry, too."

"It really bothers me that you've been so obsessed with Connor. But I figured he was dead, so he wasn't a threat to our relationship. Now I realize I was so wrong."

"How does all of this make you feel?" she asked with concern.

"To be honest, I'm shocked that the dead can communicate with us. I thought that was all a bunch of garbage. I believed that when you're dead, that's it. You're gone," he said. "I never imagined that your ex-boyfriend could die and still have some sort of a connection with you. I feel threatened and jealous. I mean, the thought of my wife's ex-boyfriend hanging around is a little unsettling—especially since he's dead. He must really love you. And I know you love him, too. So where does that leave us?"

"Dave, you don't need to worry. Yes, I love Connor. I always have. But I love you, too. I know we have our differences, but I'm not going anywhere."

"I'm glad to hear that." He smiled and gave her a big hug and a quick kiss on the lips.

Finally Dave understood what Celeste had been experiencing and had acknowledged that it was real. She was so relieved. Celeste hadn't liked the tension between her and Dave lately. Maybe now they could rekindle their relationship. There was hope for their marriage, after all.

At the office the next day, Celeste thought about how sweet Dave had been. She wanted her marriage to work. She needed a man in her life—someone she could trust, someone who would stand by her, no matter what. She smiled when she thought about how he had surprised her with flowers. Just as she thought the word "flowers," suddenly her entire office was filled with the sweet fragrance of roses. *That's weird*, she thought. *Did someone just deliver roses for a coworker?*

She opened her office door and headed down the aisle in search of the lucky recipient. But she found no roses anywhere. In fact, she no longer smelled them at all. She returned to her office. As she opened the door, again she was hit by the powerful fragrance. She thought of Connor. Was this him trying to get her attention? Celeste suddenly had an urge to see him, to meet with him again in his world.

She grabbed her purse and headed to a nearby park for lunch. She found a shady spot under a weeping willow tree and began to relax as she watched the flowing green leaves sway gently back and forth in the warm summer breeze. She closed her eyes and began her meditation. When she opened her eyes again, the bridge of illumination was lit up right in front of her, under the tree. She ran across, eager to see Connor and find out what he wanted to tell her.

She immediately saw a path surrounded by thousands of red roses petals on the ground. Connor was there, and he took her hand and led her to a white gazebo. They quietly climbed the steps together and then sat down on a bench. Connor brushed the left side of her cheek with his hand and kissed her passionately. Next he took her hand in his and held it.

Celeste watched as he got down on one knee. "No, Connor—don't!"

He looked at her with a puzzled expression.

"You're dead, and I'm already married," she explained. "You can't be proposing to me."

"Celeste," he said softly. "I wish I would have gotten married before I died. And you're the one I would have liked to marry. You're kind and sweet. You have a big heart. You're smart and beautiful. You're everything a man could ever want in a woman."

Celeste could tell that Connor believed he had missed out on something. He was trying to create a moment that he had never gotten to experience. She felt a twinge of sadness and regret. Maybe they could have been together. Maybe their relationship could have worked out. But it was too late now. Connor was dead.

She grabbed the back of his head and pulled him to her. She kissed him passionately as love filled her heart with an abundance of joy. Neither of them spoke, but no words were needed. Celeste and Connor were connected by their mutual and everlasting love. Even after death, they were powerfully drawn to each other.

Connor took her hand once again and led her to a path in the woods. This time, it was snowing. The powdery snow glittered like diamond dust in the moonlight. Celeste and Connor walked through the woods, enjoying the peacefulness and the scenery. He took off the black wool coat he was wearing and put it around her. As they reached the end of the path, Celeste was awe-struck by a huge, majestic mountain covered in sparkling, white snow. "That's incredible!" she remarked.

"Want to ski down it with me?" he asked, with that familiar, teasing grin.

"There is no way I could ever ski down *that*!" Celeste protested. "It's far too big and treacherous for me!"

"I can ski down any mountain I want," Connor said, smirking. "In the afterlife, anything is possible." A really bright golden light—kind of like the sun—began shining on them and all around them. "It was you," Connor whispered in her ear. "It's always been you."

The light became brighter and brighter, and Celeste could feel its warmth penetrating her skin. Then there was a bright flash, like fireworks on the Fourth of July. And Connor disappeared.

Celeste, back under the weeping willow tree, sat down to eat her turkey-and-swiss-cheese sandwich. All she could feel was love and peace surrounding her like a comforting fleece blanket. The love she felt wasn't for her husband. It was for the man she had let go. It was for a man who wasn't even alive on earth anymore. What a dilemma!

Instead of a husband who loved her and whom she loved, Celeste had two men in love with her. Both of them wanted to be married to her. One of them was, and one could never be. And the one she longed to be with the most was the one she could never have. Celeste felt so conflicted. Dave was a great man. He had taken good care of her and Chip. She did love him, but her feelings were not as intense and powerful as her feelings for Connor. But Connor could never be there for her the way Dave could.

Poor Dave, Celeste thought. *He's been worried*

about Connor reaching out to me. He's been concerned about losing me. And he has every reason to worry! Celeste could feel herself slipping further and further away from her husband and closer to Connor. She secretly felt guilty. Dave had no idea how Celeste had been visiting Connor's world. He would be furious if he realized that Connor wasn't just reaching out to Celeste. They were actually building a relationship together. They were sharing amazing experiences that made Celeste fall deeper and deeper in love with him. But Celeste had been faithful to Dave, hadn't she? Connor didn't have a body. He wasn't physically alive. They hadn't really done anything wrong, had they? It wasn't as if they had slept together or anything.

But still, somehow Celeste knew she had crossed a line. And there was no turning back now. She was in this too far.

***

Celeste rose early on a Saturday morning and immediately headed to the park to connect with Connor again. She had been meeting him across the bridge of illumination for months now. They had created many memories together in his world and had grown closer and closer. She always snuck out of the house to meet with Connor just before sunrise, while Dave and Chip were still sleeping. Her encounters with him left her feeling alive and exhilarated. He was like a magical happiness drug with no side effects. She could never seem to get enough of him. She only wished he were there physically so she could make passionate love with him. She could almost feel his strong body against hers as they moved together in perfect rhythm. Sex with Connor would be amazing! It was the only thing missing from their relationship.

Celeste arrived at the park and found a quiet spot to initiate her journey to the other side. She found it easier and easier to step between two worlds—her physical existence on earth and his spiritual existence in heaven.

As she traveled across the bridge, she saw twinkling stars surrounding her. The bright, yellow-orange glow of the moon lit up her path and led her directly to Connor like the North Star.

Connor smiled. He wore a white cotton shirt and twill pants. He looked casual and comfortable, like he was on a vacation. He kissed her, took her hand, and started running. They ran through the woods, and Celeste could feel the wind all around them as they ran faster and faster. Then Connor let go of Celeste's hand and had her chase him. He was laughing and smiling as they playfully ran like two rabbits in a field. They arrived at a beautiful waterfall with a rainbow overhead. He took her underneath the waterfall, and the water fell down on them, drenching their bodies like a soothing rain shower. They emerged from the waterfall soaking wet and refreshed.

Next Connor led Celeste inside some sort of lodge-type building. They settled on a tan leather sofa in front of a fireplace, Celeste sitting with Connor's arms wrapped around her from behind. The soothing warmth of the fire filled the room, and they sat mesmerized by the dancing flames.

Celeste could feel Connor's strength and comfort.

She felt completely at ease and totally safe. There was nowhere else Celeste would rather be. She was right where she belonged: in Connor's arms. Celeste lost track of time as she enjoyed the peacefulness and stillness of the present moment with Connor. She had no idea how long they sat there, just relishing each other's company. Eventually she realized she needed to get back to Dave and Chip.

Back outside, she and Connor kissed underneath the twinkling stars as they said good-bye. Celeste then headed back home.

When she walked through the door, Dave was standing there with a worried, angry look on his face. "Where the hell have you been?" he demanded.

"At the park," Celeste replied.

"Do you have any idea what time it is?"

"Actually, no," Celeste said, embarrassed.

"It's twelve fifteen! Chip and I woke up around eight, and you were gone. Be honest, Celeste. Are you having an affair?"

Celeste paused for a moment. Was this an affair? Was meeting with her former boyfriend in the spirit world a betrayal of trust? She had to try to explain all of it to Dave.

"No...I've been meeting Connor."

"What do you mean by *meeting* Connor? How is that possible? He's dead!" Celeste explained to Dave about the bridge of illumination and how she could cross it and visit with Connor. She told him how they hung out together and talked and enjoyed the beautiful scenery. She didn't have the heart to tell him how they had kissed and how uplifted she felt when she was with him.

Somehow Dave must have sensed something. "I want you to stop seeing him," he demanded. "This can't be good for you or for us. Promise me you'll stop, Celeste."

Celeste had no intention of completely giving up Connor. They had finally found each other again. She wanted him in her life, even if he could only ever be her guardian angel. She still needed him. But she also needed Dave. She wanted her marriage to work. She didn't like being alone. She wanted a secure family life.

"I can't promise anything," Celeste said. "But I will try."

"Thank you," Dave said, as he took her in his arms and gave her a big hug.

CHAPTER 15
ONENESS

Weeks passed, and Celeste hadn't visited Connor. She felt sad and empty. She and Dave had made love again, but the passion just wasn't there. She was lonely and incomplete. She desperately longed to be with Connor again. She missed him terribly, but she was trying so hard to save her marriage and keep her family together. Each day Dave would ask if she had visited Connor again. She would quietly shake her head no, and he would breathe the same sigh of relief.

One day instead of the sigh, he had a proposal. "I think we should renew our wedding vows," he offered.

"Why?" Celeste questioned, not seeing the point. "We're already married."

"We need to reaffirm our commitment to each other. I think it might help you forget about Connor and remember your vows to me."

Forget about Connor! Dave knew damn well exactly how she felt about her former love. Did Dave honestly think it was possible for her to just forget about him? Connor had become such an important part of her life. He wasn't some bad habit she could just give up. "I don't know, Dave."

"Just think about it. Please. For me and Chip?"

"Okay." She smiled weakly. But all she could really think about was Connor. Her entire being ached to be with him again. She felt like a part of her was missing, incomplete. She could stand it no longer. She had stayed away from him long enough. She just had to see him again.

That night after Dave and Chip were sleeping soundly, she quietly snuck out of the house again and headed to the park. As she was going through the relaxation and counting exercises that Star had taught her, Celeste saw an image in her mind of Connor smiling. She got the impression he was eager to communicate with her, too. After she finished her preparations and said a silent prayer, Celeste crossed the bridge of illumination and noticed there was a brilliant white light surrounding it. The light was brighter and stronger than anything she had ever seen. Celeste suspected it meant something, but she had no idea what.

Connor stood at the other end of the bridge, waiting for her. He embraced her and spun her around. Then he lifted her up and carried her. She smiled. "Where are you taking me?"

He gave her a mischievous smile of his own and began walking. He kissed her softly on the lips and then laid her down on the ground, which was covered with thousands of red and pink rose petals. Connor then gave her a gold key with a cutout heart at the top.

"What's this?" Celeste asked, puzzled.

"The key to my heart," he replied.

"Um, you don't really have a heart anymore. You're dead, remember?"

Connor laughed at this. "I may not have a physical heart, but I do have a heart and can still feel," he said. "You captured my heart and won me over." Connor looked into Celeste's eyes and continued: "I'm sorry for never telling you how I really felt about you. I didn't realize how much you meant to me until it was too late and you were already gone. Thank you for reconnecting with me. I've really missed you, Celeste."

"And I've missed you. You have no idea how much!"

Connor then took Celeste to a beautiful, tranquil lake surrounded by trees with vibrant fall colors. There was a log cabin with a boat in front of it on the lake. The two of them went into the cabin. The inside had wood walls and smelled of pine. A black bearskin rug sat in the middle of the floor in front of a brown leather sofa. A fire blazed brightly, its flames engaging in a dance of entrancement. They sat down on the couch, and Connor wrapped a multicolored, checkered blanket around both of them. They snuggled closely, feeling the security and warmth.

Just when Celeste felt totally comfortable and at ease, Connor jumped up off the couch and ran around the room. Celeste happily chased after him. He laughed playfully, coaxing her to follow him and to try to catch him. He always had liked being chased! She caught up to him in the hallway that led to the bedrooms. She grabbed his shoulders firmly, but gently. He smiled and gave her a hug.

They then returned to the living room and lay down on the soft, brown leather couch, enjoying the seclusion and coziness of this little retreat. "What are we supposed to do now?" Celeste asked.

Suddenly she felt a tingly chill, and goose bumps covered her entire body. "Can you feel me?" Connor asked. Celeste nodded in disbelief as she felt him all around her, in her, and through her. It was an unusual experience, unlike anything she had ever felt. The tingly, goose-bumps sensation continued for quite a long time. All the while, Connor explained the nature of existence to Celeste. "We are all connected—every living thing is a part of every other living thing. We are all one. We are joined together by God. We are a part of God, and he is a part of us. Always."

Connor tried to give Celeste a sense of being part of everything. She could feel him very strongly now. He was a part of her, and she was a part of him. She could feel their energies overlapping and mixing together. It was the most phenomenal experience of her life. She was filled with such unconditional love, joy, peace, and connectedness. It was truly exhilarating. She had become one with Connor and the universe.

At that point Celeste started seeing rainbow colors—blue, purple, yellow, green, pink, and orange. She got the feeling that this was significant and that it meant that when we blend together with others, we create a multitude of colors. She thought maybe that each person or spirit is like a tiny ray of light or an individual color, but together, we form a sunbeam or a rainbow. This made her think about how we are all so much more together than we could ever be separately.

She felt energized, invigorated, and happier than she had ever been in her life. It was all too much for her. Her physical body could hardly contain the all-encompassing love she was now immersed in. Her mind couldn't fully comprehend what was happening to her. "I need to go," Celeste said suddenly, feeling too much energy and emotion to continue their connection.

"What's your hurry?" Connor asked, concerned.

"This is all just too much for me," Celeste said, with tears streaming down her face. "I love you and this place more than anything. I'm afraid of being here, and I'm afraid of not being here. It's all just so overwhelming. What *was* that?"

"It's called oneness," he replied. "That's how everything is in heaven. Pure love. Pure joy. Pure exhilaration. There is no separation."

"Well, I definitely felt it," Celeste said, as she struggled to catch her breath.

"I didn't mean to frighten you. I just wanted you to understand," he continued. "I wanted you to feel what I feel. I would never do anything to hurt you. Ever since I died, I've worked hard to help you. I've done my best to protect you. All I ever wanted was for you to know the truth about everything—life, death, God, and love."

His words instantly calmed her. She looked into his warm, brown eyes. His presence entranced her. He was radiant, peaceful, and so full of love. He was more alive than she had ever been. She couldn't leave him now. She took a cleansing breath and decided to see what else

Connor had in store for her.

A white dove appeared. Celeste now wore a long, flowing, white, gauzelike dress. Connor was also dressed in all white, but in a suit. He was smiling and glowing. He looked so handsome. Celeste noticed a ring of white flowers in her hair. She was wearing them like a crown, her wavy, golden hair flowing out from it like a waterfall. The word "gardenia" came to mind, and Celeste could smell the sweet fragrance.

Connor took her hand, and they walked along the beach. He gathered up some shells and made her a shell necklace. He then handed her a bouquet of red and pink roses tied with a translucent, gold-and-white ribbon. He kissed her softly, and once again her heart overflowed with love. "Promise you'll come back?" he asked sweetly.

"I will," she replied. "Promise me you'll continue to communicate with me and help me?"

"Of course." He smiled approvingly.

Next Celeste saw a lake surrounded by green pine trees. Connor got into a small motorboat and started it up. Celeste waved good-bye. He smiled, blew her a kiss, and waved back as the boat pulled away.

She returned to the park and noticed that it was just after midnight. She had better get back home before Dave realized she was gone. Celeste hurried back to her house and quickly slipped into bed beside Dave. "You smell like roses," he said suddenly, his strong voice echoing through the room.

"What?" Celeste asked, confused.

"When you got into bed, I smelled roses."

"Oh...so what are you saying?"

161

"I'm saying I know," he said, agitation building in his voice. "I know you're seeing another man."

"What do you mean?"

"I told you not to see Connor anymore. I made you promise not to cross that bridge thingy and travel to his world. Maybe that was unfair of me. Maybe I should have been glad that you were in love with an angel and not having an affair. But no…I had to drive you further away from me! And now you really are having an affair!" he said, raising his voice. "Who is it? Your boss? Jeremy? I know he always had a thing for you. Is it one of Sue's friends? She knows a lot of guys. Please, Celeste, I'm begging you. Tell me who you're sleeping with!"

"I'm not. This isn't an affair!" she protested.

"Then what is it? You can't honestly tell me that you sneak out of the house at night to pick flowers. Who were you with?" The tone of his voice changed from angry to terrified.

"Dave, I was with Connor. I tried hard not to see him, because you asked me not to. I really want to save our marriage, but I just couldn't stay away. I'm sorry. I really missed him. Why can't you just accept that I love two men?"

"Because I want your whole heart," he said sadly. "It's all I've ever wanted."

"Is that so?" she asked sarcastically. "So is that why you work long hours and hardly ever spend any time with me?"

"No, I do that so I can give you and Chip the best of everything," he admitted. "I want you to be happy."

"Don't you know by now that I don't want *things*,

Dave? All I've ever wanted was love. I need someone who accepts me for who I am and loves me unconditionally, no matter what," Celeste cried.

"And *he* does that for you, doesn't he?"

"Yes. He always has," she admitted. "That doesn't mean there's not room in my life for you. I do think we need to change some things in order for our relationship to work, though."

"What is it, Celeste? I'll do anything to avoid losing you!" he said desperately. "Please...tell me what to do."

"For starters, you need to work less," she replied. "And no more big houses, fancy cars, or lavish gifts."

"Okay, done," he said. "What else?"

"No private schools. I want Chip to go to a regular school with his friends."

"I disagree with that decision, but I'll go along with it, if that's what you really want."

"It is. And I also want to quit my job," she continued. "I've never liked being an accountant. My true dream was always to be an artist." Dave's jaw dropped. He had thought Celeste loved her job. Who was this woman next to him in his bed? She was clearly not the person he thought she was.

"An artist? Really?" he asked, surprised. "I never even saw you draw or paint anything."

"That's because after I left Connor, I gave up that part of myself," she explained. "I tried to throw myself into a career that didn't involve feelings and creativity. I wanted something that stopped the pain, numbed my incredible loss, and healed my broken heart."

"I had no idea," Dave said, a tear slowly rolling down his cheek. "So, what you're saying is that I don't really know who you are?"

"I'm sorry, Dave...but you never really did," she said sadly. "And every time I tried to show you or voice my opinion, you didn't want to see or hear it. You wanted me to be like you and refused to see or accept anything else. I tried hard to be who you wanted me to be, but it just never felt right."

"No wonder you've been unhappy," Dave said, finally understanding. "You gave up the love of your life and wound up with a man who couldn't really give you what you wanted and needed."

She nodded in agreement, her eyes welling up with tears. Dave had hit the nail on the head.

"I may not know everything about you, Celeste, but I do know how I feel when I'm around you," he said. "I love you. I love the way you smile. I love your kind heart. I love the way you comfort Chip. I may not know what you like and don't like, but I know you're a wonderful person. I want to get to know the real you. Will you please give me a chance?"

Celeste paused and thought carefully before answering. Was this what she really wanted? Did she want to give him another chance? Dave clearly was not the right man for her, but she did marry him—for better or for worse. She decided she owed her husband an opportunity to know her better. But she knew she could never stop loving Connor, either. It wasn't really fair to Dave to have to share her. She felt guilty for even putting him in this position. On the other hand, she couldn't just turn her feelings off. She had tried that once, and it obviously didn't work. If she and Dave were going to have any kind of a future together, that future would have to include Connor. "Yes, Dave, but there's one more thing," she said.

"Anything," Dave said. "I mean that. You name it, and it's yours."

"I still want to see Connor. Please don't ask me to stop," she pleaded. "I want you to accept that he's a part of my life, kind of like a really good friend or relative. Please don't take that away from me."

"Okay," Dave said. "But when you visit him, please make sure that you behave like friends. I don't know what's possible in the spirit world, but I certainly don't want you having some sort of an otherworldly affair. I can handle you having a guardian angel or a spirit friend, as long as it's nothing more."

"Sounds fair," Celeste agreed. "But please remember that I can't stop loving him. So I hope you can learn to accept that."

"I'll try," he reluctantly agreed.

Celeste felt like she and Dave had finally gotten somewhere. All of the counseling, their separations, and their arguments had resulted in little or no progress. Tonight was definitely progress. They were heading in the right direction. Celeste was free at last to be herself and to continue seeing Connor without guilt. She would have to stop kissing him, of course. And that whole oneness experience was off-limits too. Dave would be furious if he knew about that! It would definitely be hard for her and Connor to behave like friends, but at least she would still be able to visit him.

Celeste was also thankful that Dave was willing to cut back on his hours and live a simpler life, with fewer material possessions. Their discussion tonight had been much needed. For the first time in a very long time, Celeste felt an incredible sense of hope for the future. Maybe now she could spend her life with both men she loved. Maybe she really could have it all.

CHAPTER 16
THE LESSON

*T*he next morning, Celeste awoke with a great sense of relief. She was eager to see Connor but glad she didn't have to sneak off and hide her whereabouts from Dave.

She rolled over and planted a kiss on her husband's cheek. He mumbled something about love and drifted back off. "I'm going to the park to visit with Connor," she whispered. "I'll be back in about an hour or so."

"Tell him I said hello...or is it 'halo?'" he muttered.

"Good one," she chuckled, relieved that the tension between them was gone. Celeste got dressed quickly and hurried over to the park. She wanted to tell Connor all about her breakthrough with Dave.

After she crossed the familiar bridge once again, Celeste found herself standing in front of a frozen pond at nighttime, surrounded by pine trees covered in snow.

The ground was blanketed with a soft, powdery coating. The delicate snow glistened in the moonlight, sending shimmering sparkles into the air around it.

Connor greeted Celeste with a smile and a hug. Nearby, there were a few people ice-skating. Connor took Celeste's hand and led her to the icy pond. He started skating around slowly with her. They admired the glittering snow around the pond that sparkled in the moonlight like diamond dust. Connor took great care in ensuring that Celeste didn't fall or slip on the ice. Acting as her protector, he skated at a snail's pace, being careful to maintain their balance.

Celeste, however, had other ideas. Little did Connor know, she was an ice-skating veteran. This wimpy version of skating made her laugh to herself. *He's trying to protect me and prevent me from getting hurt*, she thought. *He has no idea what I'm capable of. Time to step things up a bit!*

With that thought, she began skating faster, away from Connor. He flashed her a smile and followed, like it was some sort of chase. Celeste gave him a big, tempting grin as she increased her speed. Then, as if caught in a powerful whirlwind, she started twirling and spinning around on the ice. The wind caught her shiny, golden hair and tossed it about. She could feel the whizz of the cold air on her face and the tingling chills running through her body. She took a refreshing breath of the winter air and let the coolness fill her lungs. She felt powerful and invigorated. Celeste then leaped into the air like a bird in flight and landed a perfect double axel.

The look of surprise on Connor's face was

priceless. He'd had no idea that was coming. "Where did you learn to skate like that?" he asked.

"I loved skating at the park when I was a child." She smirked. "I would go to the ice pond every chance I got to do figure eights and spin around. My brother played hockey, so he taught me all about speed. And, my best friend was a figure skater, so she taught me a thing or two, also."

"Apparently, you had excellent teachers!" he exclaimed. Then his look turned serious as he reached for her right cheek and gently stroked her face. The moonlight reflected off her hair and lit her blue eyes up like jewels. "You are so beautiful," he said, gazing intently into her eyes. "There's so much I want to share with you. So much we missed out on in life. What would you like to do now?"

Celeste thought about her conversation last night with her husband. She knew she was supposed to just be Connor's friend now, but she just couldn't resist the temptation. Besides, Dave would never know. She didn't have to tell him. "Well, that's easy," Celeste replied with a flirty smile. "I want to experience oneness again with you. I want to feel you all through me, around me, and in me. I want to merge with you. Please touch my soul. I promise I won't be afraid this time."

"Anything for you." He smiled. "But let's go somewhere else, somewhere more special. Hold on to me and close your eyes." Celeste wrapped her arms around Connor, and he enveloped her in his. They clung to each other tightly. In an instant, Celeste noticed a subtle floating sensation and heard the soothing hum of the air all around her.

"Now open your eyes," Connor instructed. She peered into the dark night sky. The midnight-blue backdrop lit up with millions of twinkling stars. Bright white meteor showers rained down from the sky all around them. She watched in amazement as they whirred by her.

"It's breathtaking," she whispered.

"Love is the strongest and most powerful force in the universe. It is the key to everything," Connor said smiling. "It can never be destroyed. When people pass away, they leave the earth. They don't leave you. Their love continues, even brighter and stronger than before. The love from the afterlife rains down on the earth just like these radiant meteor showers."

Celeste's eyes filled with tears. But this time, they were no longer tears of sorrow or sadness; they were tears of joy, gratitude, and love.

"Thank you...for all that you've shown me and everything you've taught me," she said, admiring both his wisdom and charm. "For the first time, I think I finally grasp the magnitude of love and its all-encompassing power. You've given me the greatest gift I could ever ask for."

"I'm not done yet," he said with a wink. "Now turn around."

The night sky faded from view, and everything basked in a brilliant sunlight. It was then that Celeste saw an incredible sight. Majestically standing in the middle of a beautiful field of purple and yellow wildflowers stood a radiant, golden, pyramidlike palace. It appeared to be made of pure, polished gold, intricately carved with an elegant pattern of stars and moons. The shiny surface reflected the colors of the flowers surrounding it like a mirror. Pristinely polished, white marble steps led up to the pyramid. Celeste had never before seen such a gorgeous, mighty structure.

Connor took her hand again, and together they climbed the glossy steps, one by one. Neither spoke a word. They were too caught up in the splendor of the moment.

When they finally reached the top, Connor touched the surface of the palace, and a door slid open. They entered, and the door closed swiftly behind them. Inside, the entire palace was tiled in beige and white marble and trimmed in the brightest, most glittering gold. Within the gold trim were diamonds of all shapes and sizes. The ceiling was made of stained glass in a beautiful, mosaic pattern of rainbow colors. At the peak of the ceiling, a radiant beam of pure white light shone down into the center of the room.

Connor led Celeste to a room inside the pyramid. It too had shiny marble floors and walls, but instead of gold and diamonds, this room was filled with thousands of lush, vibrant-red roses. The sweet fragrance surrounded the room like a warm embrace. In the very center, on a raised marble platform, was a king-size bed draped with a champagne satin comforter. When Celeste saw it, her heart stopped. "Connor, I can't do this. I'm married," she said.

"Don't worry," he said softly. "This isn't sex. I don't have a body, and I have no physical urges to do that anymore."

"Then what are we going to do?"

"You'll see. Just lay down on the bed."

Celeste trusted Connor with her life and knew he would never do anything to hurt her, so she quietly complied. She lay there completely still as Connor stood at the foot of the bed, watching her. She admired his wavy, brown hair and compassionate, brown eyes. He gave her a charming smile, and her heart just melted. Her love for him had grown stronger since he died. She wanted him totally and completely. But as he had said, he didn't have a body. And she was married. Besides, she had promised Dave last night that she and Connor would just be friends. She had really missed the boat on this one!

"Now, close your eyes," Connor instructed.

Celeste did as he asked, lying there silently in anticipation, waiting for whatever was next. Ordinarily, she would be afraid of being so vulnerable, but instead she found herself strangely and pleasantly intrigued.

First she noticed a gentle breeze drift across her body. Next was a soft touch that tickled her left cheek, like the brush of a feather. Then she felt a soft caress on her left leg. Celeste felt so peaceful and relaxed.

The energy in the room changed and became stronger. It was no longer just peaceful; all around her, Celeste could feel a powerful, soothing force of unconditional love. It was intense and energizing, yet gentle. And inside herself, Celeste was overflowing with abundant joy. She wanted to sing out, celebrate, laugh, and weep, all at the same time. Never in her life had she experienced such happiness.

Connor lay down on the bed beside her. The feelings continued to build until Connor's and Celeste's spirits joined together again, overlapping and surrounding each other. Celeste felt electrified. A bright explosion of light illuminated the room like the grand finale of a fireworks display on the Fourth of July. Suddenly Celeste was no longer Celeste, and Connor was no longer Connor. They just were.

The earth...the moon...the stars...the sky...all of the universe was a part of them, and they were part of it. They were one once again. Everything was connected in pure love.

Celeste let out a gasp, and tears streamed down her cheeks. She was a changed woman. She knew that she could never love anything or anyone more than this. The experience, the place, Connor, everything around her—it was all sheer bliss.

As the intensity of the feelings built, Connor moved over her and their spirits aligned perfectly. He kissed her lips passionately, and she fervently responded. She knew that his kiss was forbidden, but she was powerless to stop it. Being in his presence made her want him even more. She had always wanted him, but never like this. This was so much more satisfying. She really felt him. He was a part of her. Their souls were intertwined in pure love. How could this be wrong when it felt so right? "I love you, Connor," she said. "I have always loved you, and I always will—no matter what."

"I feel the same way," he said, gently stroking her soft hair.

The oneness then dissipated, and Celeste felt like her usual, separate self again. Although she had lived this way all of her life, it now felt strangely foreign to her.

"C'mon," Connor said teasingly as he attempted to lighten the mood. He knew how incomplete she was now feeling. "Follow me."

Without a second thought, Celeste rose from the bed and followed Connor out of the room and through another golden door. They were now standing outside, surrounded by an incredible beach scene. Both of them wore bathing suits. He sported navy-blue swim shorts, and she was in a two-piece, yellow bikini. Connor started running barefoot through the soft, beige sand, and she playfully ran after him. Then he threw a blue Nerf football at her. "Cute, Connor." She smirked. "But I actually like Frisbees better!" He then tossed a yellow Frisbee her way, and she happily flung it back to him. They continued their game for several minutes, enjoying the warm sun, gentle breeze, and crystal-clear, blue sky.

Next they ran into the water, laughing, splashing, and frolicking in the waves. Connor started swimming. Celeste watched as he swiftly glided across the lake, almost effortlessly, and then swam back to her. "You're a very good swimmer," Celeste complimented him.

"You mean Miss Ice-Skating Queen doesn't swim?" he teased.

"I swim. My best stroke is the doggy paddle." She laughed. Connor then picked Celeste up and tossed her into the water. She emerged quickly, streams of water running down her face from her drenched, tousled hair.

"I'm really *not* a very good swimmer," she warned.

"That's okay." He smiled. "Climb on my shoulders, and I'll help you get around in the water."

Celeste happily climbed on Connor's back. She could feel the power of his strong, protective arms wrapped around hers. He began walking through the water, with Celeste riding prominently on his shoulders.

Then he caught her by surprise as he sank down and quickly dunked Celeste underwater. "Hey!" she cried as she rose from the waves, soaking wet once again.

He laughed a joyful, hearty laugh. He always did enjoy teasing her. Connor was so happy to be able to spend some quality time with the only woman he had ever really loved.

After they had spent some time in the water, the sky changed. It was no longer broad daylight. Now, a beautiful, orange-and-pink sunset hung over the water. The light glistened and reflected off of the waves. Connor and Celeste just stood there watching and admiring the scene. "It sure is gorgeous," Celeste said softly.

"Just like you," he replied as he reached behind his back, magically retrieving a crystal necklace. As he put it around her neck, a rainbow of colors projected out from it.

"Thank you," she said, planting a wet kiss on his lips.

"You're very welcome." He beamed. Connor walked over to a nearby rock and picked up a yellow notepad and pen. Celeste found that a bit odd. They had just had an extraordinary experience of oneness and were having an awesome day at the beach. What was with the notepad? It didn't seem to fit. She watched as Connor sat down on the rock and wondered what was next. "Time to get to work," he announced.

"Work?" Celeste asked, perplexed. "But I'm having so much fun! I don't want this to end."

He became very serious and gave her a stern look. Celeste got the feeling she was about to get a lesson or lecture of some sort. "There are some very important things I want you to always remember," he started.

"Okay."

Connor began writing on the paper with a blue ballpoint pen. First he drew a small star, followed by a list of words below it. It wasn't any ordinary list; each phrase was built upon the next one to form what resembled steps, just like the ones they had climbed to reach the top of the golden pyramid palace. Celeste's mind wandered back to the palace, that glorious sacred place where she could feel the universal love of God and all of creation. She longed to return there again... "Please pay attention," Connor urged, snapping her back to the present moment.

Celeste watched him as he intently etched the words that climbed to the star. She was amazed at the change in Connor. He was not his playful self. He no longer seemed like her friend, her lover, or her soul mate. Right now he was her teacher, her mentor. And, he was determined to get an important message across. Celeste knew that, as a person in spirit, Connor must possess a knowledge and awareness of things far beyond her comprehension. He had become enlightened when he crossed over to the other side. He had naturally acquired some of the universal wisdom of the Creator. Now he was trying to share a small part of his newfound wisdom with her. Connor wanted Celeste to have a greater understanding of life and the way the universe operated. He wanted to help her live a better, richer, more rewarding life on earth. He had been working with her since he had passed to help her achieve this.

When Connor finished writing the last phrase, he

handed the notebook to Celeste. She read:

Let go
Believe
Have faith
Love deeply
Let me guide you
Experience peace
Trust your intuition
Give freely of yourself
Know that you are beautiful
Ask for help when you need it
Trust the natural process of life
Know that I am always here with you

He had given her useful, practical advice on how to live a better life! He was teaching and guiding her from the afterlife. She wanted to say something, to thank him, but she found no words to express her gratitude. All she could manage was a sweet smile. She silently stood before him, captivated by his energy and wisdom and their everlasting, loving connection.

Connor didn't speak, either. He just kissed her gently on the forehead, smiled, jumped into the water, and swam away.

CHAPTER 17
THE CHANGE

"You seem different, Mommy," Chip observed as he munched on buttered toast, scrambled eggs, and sausage.

"What do you mean, honey?"

"Well, you're happier. And you look even prettier than before," he explained. "Is it because of the angel?"

"You mean, Connor?"

"Yeah. I really like him. He's a funny guy. And he's nice, too. And a good swimmer. He can do more than just the doggy paddle."

"How do you know all of that, Chip?"

"He visited me again," Chip happily explained.

"Oh?"

"Yeah. He told me that he's gonna teach me how to swim, since all Mommy knows is the doggy paddle. He also said that he is my guardian angel, too! Isn't that so cool?"

"Yes, it is." Celeste grinned. "What else did he say to you?"

"Just that he loves you. And that you're not supposed to be with Daddy. He said Daddy is going to leave again. Is that true?"

"No, Daddy isn't leaving. He just got back. Besides, he loves me, too!"

"I know, but Connor said that there's no going back now," Chip said. "God's plan has been put into motion."

Celeste felt a wave of fear as her son spoke these words. What did that mean? Why was Connor telling her son these things? He hadn't said anything to her. "Just because Connor's an angel doesn't mean he knows everything," Celeste snapped, feeling angry at Connor for interfering in her son's life.

"Don't worry, Mommy," Chip said soothingly. "Connor said no matter what happens, he will be there to guide and protect me. And he said I have the best mom in the world and that you'll always look out for me, even when we're apart."

"Apart? As in, you're at Daddy's new house without *me*?" Celeste snapped.

"Not sure. He didn't say." Chip shrugged.

"Well, it sure sounds like he said plenty!"

"Maybe he means while I'm at school or at Grandma's house?" Chip offered. "By the way, where is Daddy?"

"Oh, he went to the office early this morning. Something about an acquisition."

"I miss him." Chip sighed.

"Yeah, I know," Celeste said, realizing that she

actually didn't miss her husband at all. In fact, it hardly fazed her that he was gone. It just seemed like a natural, normal thing. She was used to his absence. Were she and Dave really going to get divorced? Things had seemed so much better with them since last night. Was Connor right about Dave leaving her?

They might have their differences, but Celeste still needed her husband. He was a great companion, father, and provider. Why would he leave her? He had wanted so much to get back together with her. He had said he would do anything for her. "You tell Connor next time you see him that he needs to talk to *me* about these things," Celeste said sharply, feeling a cold chill rush across her shoulders.

"Why don't you tell him yourself?" Chip suggested. "He's standing right behind you."

Celeste suddenly felt an overwhelming sense of love and peace. Then she clearly heard Connor's voice in her head: "I'm sorry. I didn't mean to upset you. Those words weren't meant for you; they were meant for Chip. I was trying to prepare him."

"Prepare him for what? My divorce?" she asked.

"I'm sorry. I can't tell you. I'm not allowed to divulge secrets about the future."

"But you just did, to Chip!" she protested.

"That's different. It was necessary," he answered. "Trust me. One day, you'll understand everything. Now is not the time."

Celeste felt herself calming down more and more. Maybe there was a plan or a purpose to all of this. She knew Connor would never do anything to hurt her. "Okay, I do trust you," she said. "And I forgive you.

And I love you!"

"Thank you. I'll be in touch," he said as he slowly faded from sight. "I love you, too…"

Celeste stood there in the kitchen, not sure what to think. The morning sunlight was now peeking in through the venetian blinds, creating a warm, happy glow on the yellow walls. Inside she felt the lingering comfort of Connor's presence, but a part of her was confused by what he had said. She wanted answers. Why couldn't Connor just be up-front with her? Had God told him he had to keep this secret?

"Mommy, you and the angel should get married!" Chip announced, interrupting her train of thought.

"First of all, you can't marry an angel." Celeste laughed. "And secondly, I'm already married to your dad. You can't marry two people."

"Well, if Daddy leaves, then you'll need a new husband," Chip explained. "And I pick Connor for my second daddy!"

"Sorry to disappoint you, Chip, but that's not going to happen."

"But you love each other!" Chip exclaimed. "When two people love each other that much, don't they get married?"

"Sadly, no, life doesn't always work that way. Sometimes two people madly in love don't ever get married. Other times, people who don't love each other at all do get married. And then there are those who marry for all the wrong reasons, such as money, or because they think they'll never find anyone else."

"That's just messed up!" Chip said.

"Yeah, the world doesn't always work the way it

should," she agreed.

"But Connor says in heaven, everything is perfect. There is so much love. No fights. No wars. No yelling. Just love. And everyone is happy!"

"Connor's right," Celeste agreed, as she remembered what it felt like to be there with him. "Heaven is a remarkable place. Now let's finish breakfast and get dressed!"

CHAPTER 18
DEPARTURE

*F*all had arrived once again, and little Chip was now in school. Since Celeste had quit her job as an accountant, she now had more free time to pursue her dreams of becoming an artist and visit with Connor. Her life had been transformed and enriched.

Celeste happily crossed the bridge of illumination, ready to meet with Connor again. She was in a good mood. Her sadness had faded tremendously since Connor's passing a year ago. After all, what did she have to be sad about? Not only was he doing well in the afterlife, she could now visit him there whenever she wanted. It wasn't the same as having him physically present, but it was definitely a wonderful and miraculous experience. And he had been teaching her so much about how the universe really worked and how to improve her own life. She was thankful for these incredible moments with him.

As Celeste reached the other side of the bridge, Connor stood there patiently waiting for her, looking happier and more radiant than ever. He was wearing a crisp, white, button-front shirt and blue jeans. He smiled that familiar charming grin she had always loved. Apparently, heaven really agreed with him!

Connor embraced her warmly and guided her to their first destination. Celeste saw a beautiful waterfall gently cascading over an iridescent rock formation. Nearby was a rushing river. The water was so clear and sparkling. It was the purest water she had ever seen. Celeste was always so entranced by the glorious beauty of the world beyond. Just when she thought there couldn't possibly be anything more gorgeous, Connor showed her something ever better. Heaven was even more spectacular than she had imagined.

"Come on." Connor smiled, taking Celeste's hand. "I have more to show you." He seemed extra excited today, and Celeste sensed that there was something big and special coming. She just didn't know what.

They then arrived at a fancy, outdoor courtyard with a shiny, beige marble floor framed by white stone steps. Connor and Celeste sat on the steps together, and he took out a small, brown leather book. There was a magnificent, golden glow all around it. Celeste wondered if there were more lessons inside. What was he going to teach her today? She couldn't wait to learn more. He quietly handed her the book. Much to her surprise, when Celeste opened it and flipped through the pages, they were blank. She was confused.

Then she heard the words: "Write your own

story." She couldn't tell where the voice had come from, so she assumed it must be God. Celeste then thought about how we all create our own lives based on what we think, feel, and choose to do. She remembered how our lives can be whatever we want them to be. Our thoughts shape our reality. We literally have the power to write our own stories.

"You learn fast," Connor said proudly, reading her mind again. He then took the empty book and wrote something in it before handing it back to her. Celeste opened it and read: *I love you.* She turned the page and read: *I will always love you.*

"I love you too, Connor." Celeste beamed. She didn't understand why he was writing it down on paper, though. It was very sweet and touching, but there must be more to it. What was he trying to accomplish here?

"I have to go now," he said seriously.

"What? What do you mean? Where are you going?" Celeste asked, obviously alarmed. She realized that her meeting with Connor today had felt a lot like a good-bye. She didn't want him to go. Celeste had become accustomed to their regular meetings. She loved having Connor in her life again. "Please don't. I don't want you to go," Celeste pleaded.

"I have to," he replied firmly.

Connor then showed her an image of himself wearing a glowing, green robe. He said he had advanced to the "next level." Celeste got the impression that he was able to move up in part because of his work with her. Connor had helped her and taught her so much since his passing. Apparently, souls earn brownie points for that in the afterlife. But did that mean he had to leave permanently? She still needed him. She didn't want to lose him again.

An older gentleman appeared. He had white hair and was wearing a glowing, white robe with a gold sash. He looked very kind and wise. Celeste thought that this was probably Connor's teacher or mentor. This elderly man must be the person who was taking Connor away somewhere.

Celeste, with tears in her eyes, wanted to know if she would see Connor again one day. The man didn't speak, but Celeste got the impression that Connor's absence would be temporary. Still, she was feeling very sad and wanted more answers. How temporary? Days? Weeks? Months? Years? She just couldn't bear that!

She said once again that she didn't want him to go. She wanted to know when she would see him again. Celeste was desperate, practically begging someone to tell her. She prayed to God, asking for his guidance and assistance. But there was no response. Neither the man nor Connor seemed to know the details of Connor's departure or when he would return. All they knew was that Connor needed to prepare for his mission. God had instructed the man to come and get him today.

"I need to know when I will see him again. Please," Celeste sobbed, tears streaming down her face.

A booming voice projected all around her. "Someday," it answered.

She realized that this was it. The situation was completely out of her control. It was in God's hands now. She had to let Connor go. With tears streaming down her face, Celeste reluctantly said: "Good-bye, Connor." She thanked him for his help. She could hardly get the words out, feeling so emotional. She told Connor she really didn't want to let go of him and to please come back and see her again sometime, as soon as he was able. "Please, Connor, at least send me more songs and signs," she pleaded.

"Remember what I taught you," Connor reminded Celeste. He showed her the image of the lesson with the pyramid steps. He then took her into his arms and hugged her with the strongest, most loving embrace she had ever felt. He kissed her tenderly, handed her a delicate red rose, and then disappeared.

Connor was out of her life once again. Celeste felt lost and empty. She sobbed into her hands. Why had God allowed her to get so close to him, only to take him away again?

CHAPTER 19
ALONE AGAIN

*C*eleste awoke the next morning with a horrible headache. Her whole body felt heavy and sore. There was a persistent ache in the center of her chest. She was experiencing true heartache. Connor had left. She felt like he had died all over again. What was she going to do?

Dave rolled over and planted a kiss on her cheek. At least she still had her husband and son. Otherwise, Celeste really would be alone. "Good morning, sweetheart!" Dave said cheerily.

"Morning," Celeste groaned.

As Dave took a good look at her, he immediately realized something was wrong. "Celeste, you look terrible! What the hell happened to you?"

"Nothing. Really. I'm fine."

"You are not fine. Are you sick or something? Were

you out drinking last night? Something happened to you. I can tell. Please tell me what it is."

"No, I'm not sick or hung over," Celeste replied.

"Then what is it?" Dave studied Celeste's eyes and expression. He saw a sadness he hadn't seen in a long time. Celeste looked heartbroken, as if someone she loved had died. Then it dawned on him. This must have to do with Connor. "It's him, isn't it?" Dave asked with his familiar jealous tone. "Did you see him again last night? What happened between you two? You're supposed to just be friends. People don't look like that when they're in a friendship with someone, Celeste."

Dave had gotten used to Celeste thinking about Connor, although he was still uncomfortable with the visits. He sensed that something more was going on, even though he had asked Celeste to make sure their relationship was strictly a friendship. The guy might be dead, but he obviously still loved Dave's wife, and she loved him too. Dave certainly didn't want to lose Celeste to a ghost.

"Yes, I did see him last night. We had a good visit, but now he's gone. Connor went away."

"Oh, good. That's probably for the best. Maybe he'll leave you alone now," Dave said, feeling relieved. "Maybe now we can finally rebuild our relationship and our lives together."

"You really don't care, do you?" Celeste asked, tears streaming down her face.

"I get it. The guy died. It's sad. His ghost came to make you feel better. End of story."

"No, Dave. It's not the end of the story. I really love him. I can't bear the thought of being without him. I feel like I've lost a piece of myself. He's a part of me, and I'm a part of him."

"The ghost? What the hell, Celeste? I'm your husband! You're supposed to love me that way!"

"I do love you, just in a different way. It's possible to love more than one person, you know."

"Not for me," Dave said dryly. "Did something happen with him? Did you make love somehow? Did he touch you?"

"Spirits don't have sex," she said.

"Well, that's a relief!" Dave replied.

"But yes, he did touch me. It was the most beautiful experience of my life," she continued. "It was as if our souls overlapped and mixed together to form one. It wasn't about anything physical; it was just pure love."

"Sure sounds like sex to me, Celeste," Dave said, his blood boiling. "So essentially, you cheated on me with him after you promised you would just be friends. Somehow he found a way to make you his. You and Connor betrayed me!"

"No, it wasn't like that at all," said Celeste. "You see, every living being is a part of the universe. We are all connected together as one. We are parts of a whole. It isn't about Connor or me or you. It's about God. It's about love. It's about harmonic resonance."

"Harmonic what?"

"Harmonic resonance. It's when two energies vibrate at the same frequency. That's what makes it possible to communicate with those who have passed. Connor and I achieved harmonic resonance. It's like we were on the same exact wavelength."

"So you're saying you and Connor are vibrating together in perfect harmony?" Dave said angrily.

"Yes. That's part of the beauty of life. When you achieve that level of vibration, the world becomes a richer, more loving, more beautiful place. You connect in ways you could never imagine were possible."

"So are you saying that you and Connor are soul mates?" Dave asked, feeling his wife slipping away. He couldn't believe this was happening. How could someone who died have this effect on her?

"Sort of. But we are so much more than that. We are parts of the whole. Like bricks that join together to form a wall. Or individual cells that are all working together in one body."

"From everything you're saying, it still sounds like you and Connor made love. All this talk about joining together, vibrating, and experiencing pure love—isn't that what sex is? Isn't that what a man and a woman physically do together?"

"Sometimes. But what Connor and I shared...it goes far beyond anything physical. It is pure spiritual energy. It is complete and total love. And I'm not just talking about between Connor and me. I'm talking about between us and everything."

Dave could feel his jealousy and rage building by the moment. Celeste kept saying that she and Connor hadn't made love. But what she was describing sounded like sheer ecstasy. It sounded like something that every couple strives to achieve in their relationship. And she had experienced it with *him*! How could he be with a woman who was, as she put it, mixed together as one with another being? It was bad enough that Dave only ever had part of Celeste's heart. Now he had to share her soul, too? He couldn't imagine their relationship ever being anything more than just a partnership. Heart and soul, she belonged to Connor. He was so angry with both of them. How could they do this to him? The woman he loved, and a man who no longer even lived on earth? Celeste and Connor weren't supposed to be able to be together. Yet somehow they were more together than Dave and Celeste had ever been. She had fully and completely given herself to another man. She had no regrets, no guilt, no apologies. She was radiant and blissfully happy about it. She stood there in front of her husband and described this amazing relationship she had with her ex-boyfriend's ghost—a relationship that Dave could never compete with. Is this why he always felt like he was swimming upstream, against the current, with Celeste? Their relationship had always seemed to be a struggle, an uphill battle. Nothing was ever easy, natural, or effortless for them. Was it because she was meant to be with Connor? Clearly they were still strongly connected, even after Connor's death. He realized now they always would be. There was nothing left for him to do now but let her go.

He had never thought it would come to this. Somehow he had expected them to work out their differences and one day thrive as a couple. She had married him, after all. They had exchanged vows. They had pledged to forsake all others and to love each other until death parted them. Maybe he wasn't good at this whole love thing. Perhaps he did spend too much time at the office. Maybe he was self-absorbed at times and too materialistic. He had to admit that he had always been jealous of her friendships with other men. It was also true that he hadn't taken the time to get to know her or really listen to what she wanted. He knew he had screwed up. But that didn't mean that gave her the right to join her soul with another man. That was still a breach of trust! He had trusted her, and she'd betrayed him. How could she? "That's it! I've had it, Celeste. We're through," he said angrily as he took off his wedding ring and slammed it down on the nightstand.

"No, Dave!" Celeste cried. "Don't do this. I do love you. I never meant to hurt you. I still need you."

"Really, Celeste?" he said sarcastically. "What could I ever possibly give you that he hasn't already given you?"

"A real life on earth. A father to my child. A friend and partner. Someone to come home to every night."

"Sorry, babe. I just can't share you with him. You belong to Connor. As much as I tried to deny it, you've always belonged to him. Your heart and your soul were with him all along. From the moment I met you, I instinctively knew this. I just refused to give up. I was determined to make you forget about him and make you really love me. I was accustomed to winning and succeeding at every endeavor I've ever undertaken. But this time, I failed. The love between you and Connor is just too strong. Nothing—and no one—can ever come between you two. I see that now. It makes me furious, but I can't do a damn thing about it. Good-bye, Celeste."

And with those words, he headed to the living room, opened the door and walked out of her life.

Celeste followed behind, calling after him, but he ignored her. She collapsed onto the living room couch and burst into tears. Yesterday Connor had been taken away from her. And today her husband had left her for good. She had truly lost everything. The love of her life was gone to who-knows-where in the spiritual realms. The father of her child no longer wanted any sort of a relationship with her. How could this be happening?

She understood how Dave felt. He was right about her feelings for Connor. It had been selfish of her to think she could have both a husband and a true love. But she really did care about Dave. And now she was more alone than she had ever been in her life.

She wondered why everything was falling apart. All the experiences she had encountered with after-death communication, travels to the other world, love, learning, and spiritual enlightenment must have meant *something*. That couldn't have all been for nothing. So why had it turned out this way? What was she supposed to do now? Where was this elusive "soul purpose" that Star Walker had told her about?

Through her sobs, she heard a strong knock at the door. Had Dave changed his mind? She jumped from the couch and ran to the door. When she opened it, she was shocked to see Andy staring back at her. "Hellooo, hot stuff," he said with a wicked smile. "Ready to finish what we've started?"

Fear pierced through Celeste's heart as she realized that she had no one left to protect her now. Connor and Dave were gone, and she was standing face-to-face with her biggest nightmare. How would she ever get out of this one? "Hi, Andy. This isn't a good time," she said, wiping away tears.

"I know. Your husband left you," he said with a

gleam in his eyes. "I heard him yelling and saw him leave in a huff."

"Were you spying on me?"

"Not spying, just watching. Observing. You know, waiting for the perfect moment."

"Andy, that's called stalking, you know," she said.

"Oooh, your words hurt me, Celeste. Do you have any idea what I've been through to be with you? I'd move mountains to make you mine. Hell, I'd even take down a plane to eliminate the competition."

"What did you say?" Celeste asked.

"About moving mountains?"

"No, about a plane."

"Oh, yeah, that. It was actually pretty tricky. I heard Connor was coming back, and I had to make sure you two never hooked up again. I knew if you so much as looked into each other's eyes, it would be all over for me. So I bought a plane ticket to Rome and paid off an airplane mechanic to tamper with Connor's plane. Genius, wasn't it?"

Celeste could feel the tears welling up in her eyes. Andy had been responsible for the plane crash. He had killed Connor! She knew he was jealous, possessive, and abusive, but she had never deemed him a killer! She had to get away from this man before he hurt her. But she knew that being angry wouldn't work. She needed to be kind and gentle with him. That was the only time Andy ever let down his guard. He loved to be praised and babied, like a young child. "Andy," she said with a sweet tone. "You're such a devoted man. To think you loved me that much!"

"I know, isn't it heartwarming?" he asked proudly.

"I'm not sure heartwarming is the right word," she said, still managing to keep her cool. "Killing another human being is just plain wrong, after all."

"I know, I've been a very bad boy, haven't I?" he admitted. "But I did it for you! That's gotta count for something, right?"

Secretly she wanted to rip his heart out for what he had done to Connor. But she knew that violence and hatred were never the answer. Connor had taught her that love was the only thing that really could conquer all. As long as you have love in your heart, anything is possible. So Celeste took a deep breath and concentrated on her love for Connor. He wasn't here now. But she could still feel him. He was a part of her. His strength was her strength. "I have an idea, Andy," she said as she planted a kiss on his cheek. "I want to give you something."

"Ooh, a gift?" he said, like a kid in a candy store.

"A little something from me to you," she said secretively. "But I have to go get it."

"Okay," he said. "But hurry back. I can't wait to make you mine again."

"I'll only be a minute," said Celeste reassuringly. "Just sit down here on the porch swing and make yourself at home."

Andy did as she suggested. He looked content and less agitated. Now was the time for Celeste to make her escape. She discreetly fetched her keys and cell phone from her purse, and slowly and confidently headed around the side of the house. She looked back to see if Andy was watching. He wasn't. She then bolted down the street like a flash of lightning.

As she ran, she pulled her cell phone from her pocket and called 911. "Hello? There's a man after me. I'm running down Prescott Street. He killed my ex-boyfriend and tried to rape me. My son is sleeping in the house alone. Please send help."

As she completed her call, she heard the screech of tires behind her. She turned to find Andy speeding toward her in his shiny, red convertible Corvette. He looked angry. Andy pulled up alongside of her and rolled down the window. "Celeste, you disappoint me," he said. "How could you do this to me?"

"Do this to you?" she replied angrily. "You beat me, killed the love of my life, and tried to rape me. I'd say I'm the victim in all of this!"

"You were never the victim. You wanted me just as much as I wanted you."

"No, Andy, I didn't. Don't the words 'please stop, you're hurting me' mean anything to you?"

❊ ❊ ❊

Andy paused and didn't know what to say. Suddenly images of his childhood flashed through his head. His angry, drunken father beating him with a baseball bat while his mother sat and watched. Being chained to his own bed for three hours because he hadn't finished his vegetables. A tiny five-year-old child crying and begging *Please, Daddy, don't hurt me.* Was that how Celeste had felt? Had he inadvertently become his father? Had his worst nightmare come true?

No, he wasn't like his father—he truly loved Celeste. His dad was incapable of love. Besides, Celeste loved him too, didn't she? Wasn't that why she was always nice to him? "Do you still love me, Celeste?"

"Andy, I feel compassion for you. I feel sorry for you. I know that you were hurt once. I know you don't really want to hurt me. But I'm not *in* love with you. I love Connor."

She loved *him*. He was dead and buried. And she still wanted *him*. But Connor couldn't have her anymore. She belonged to Andy now. There was no one standing in his way anymore. Nothing could stop him from making her his once again. "Get in the car, Celeste," Andy demanded.

"No, Andy, I'm not going anywhere with you," Celeste replied firmly. She took off running once again. Andy rolled up the window and floored it. In a moment of jealous rage, he aimed the car directly at Celeste. If he couldn't have her, no one could.

He watched numbly as the car struck her body, flipping her over the hood of his car like a limp rag doll. He heard her screams upon impact; then there was a deadening silence. He stared numbly at the blood streaking the windshield. Celeste was gone for good.

Andy thought he would feel some sense of relief, but that wasn't how he felt at all. He had expected he would feel powerful and in charge, but he felt neither. He was weak. He was empty. He was alone. He had no one left to help him. Andy sat motionless in his mangled car. For the first time in his life, he felt remorse. He had killed the woman he loved. He was truly a monster, just like his father. He didn't deserve Celeste. He didn't even deserve to be here.

The piercing sound of emergency sirens filled the

still air. Andy remained frozen in his car, unable to do anything. He awaited his fate. He welcomed a life of imprisonment. It really wouldn't be any different from his regular life; only now, he wouldn't be able to hurt anyone. The world would be safe from Andy. Maybe one day, he would be saved as well.

CHAPTER 20
JOINING FORCES

*E*verything faded to black.

Moments later, Celeste awoke with a very light and dreamy sensation. Her eyes were still closed, but she became aware of a subtle, floating sensation, like she was slowly drifting through the air. Her body felt no pain or fear, only quietness, stillness, and peace. She opened her eyes to observe her surroundings. Glittering stars and beams of radiant light encircled her. She was overcome by feelings of joy and love. What had happened? Where was she? Was this some kind of dream?

Just as those thoughts entered her mind, she noticed something glowing in the distance. It was the bridge of illumination. She drifted toward it like a breeze gently blowing on a warm spring day. As she approached the bridge, it became surrounded with a luminescent, white glow. At the base of the bridge were the most gorgeous wildflowers imaginable, in vibrant shades of red, yellow, blue, pink, and orange. She stepped on the bridge, and suddenly the white glow turned into a beautiful shade of pink, like the color of a sunrise at dawn. She was completely and totally mesmerized by the beauty all around her. During her journeys to the other world, she had never seen any of this happen before. She didn't know what it meant, but she was magnetically drawn to the other side of the bridge by a powerful, enchanting force. The energy was magnificent. She felt as if she were a part of the bridge, the light, and the flowers. This wasn't just a crossway to the other side; it was a part of her essence, her being.

Celeste reached the end of the bridge and drifted through a soft, pink, hazy cloud that emitted the faint scent of roses until everything suddenly became crystal clear. She arrived at a stunning outdoor garden scene. The focal point was a white trellis intricately woven into a delicate diamond pattern. The trellis was covered with fragrant roses in the purest shade of white. On the ground were white flowers of every kind imaginable— gardenias, carnations, freesias, stephanotis, gladiolus, and lilies. Among the flowers, she spotted her relatives: her beloved grandparents, her father, and her cousin. All had passed many years ago. They were smiling at her, and she could feel their welcoming love flowing through her like a river.

Connor stood before her, smiling and dressed in a white suit. Celeste noticed that she was now wearing a flowing, layered white dress covered in shimmering crystals that reflected the light.

Connor took both of Celeste's hands and then kissed her gently. She closed her eyes and felt his loving energy and compassion run through her. When she opened her eyes again, her relatives were gone, but Connor remained. She saw a large pond with a cascading fountain in the center of it. The water was a glittery shade of azure. Two mallard ducks swam across the pond, and a white dove landed on the water. Celeste then saw two white swans float together so their heads and necks formed a heart. She felt a sense of love, joy, and accomplishment and wondered if this was some sort of special occasion. But she was too astonished to speak.

Was this heaven? And if it was, where was God? Where were the pearly gates she had heard so much about? Where were the harps and winged angels?

A booming voice that appeared to emanate from all directions said: "Yes, Celeste, this is heaven. You can't see God. You can only feel him. He's not a person looking down from the sky ready to reward or punish you. God is a powerful energy source that is all around you and present in all things. God is a part of you, and you are a part of God. That's why people on earth say that you are never alone and that the Lord is always with you. On some level, they understand that God can never leave us. However, they fail to realize the scope and magnitude of it all. The truth is: he's with you because he *is* you. We are all part of the Divine. It's how we began and how we will always be—intricately connected to both God and each other. We are one."

Wow. That's pretty profound, Celeste thought. *This sure is an incredible dream. I hope I remember it when I wake up.*

Next Celeste saw shimmering, white stone steps that reminded her of freshly fallen snow sparkling in the moonlight. The steps stretched way up into the sky and disappeared into the clouds. Several people were climbing the steps, but she couldn't see where they were going. Connor took her hand and silently led her to the steps. They slowly and purposefully climbed them together.

When they reached the top, there were beams of rainbow colors projecting out in all directions from a center point. Celeste then saw a beam of pure white light coming from a star. Then the older gentleman with whitish-grey hair and a white robe with gold trim appeared. The man placed a headpiece with an emerald-green stone in the center of it on Celeste's head. The headpiece was woven with gold threads and went around the back of her head. The stone adorned her forehead.

The man waved his hands around in circular, rhythmic motions, and Celeste got the impression he was conducting a ceremony. He then put some type of bronze medal around Connor's neck that had the same green stone in it. The medal glowed and hung directly over his heart. Celeste remembered that the last time she had seen the white-haired man, she had been forced to say good-bye to Connor. She started to fear that the man was going to take Connor away again. She couldn't let that happen. For the first time since she had arrived in this magical place, she spoke. "I don't want to lose you," she said to Connor.

"You're not going to lose me," he said comfortingly, stroking her shoulder with his hand. "You've found me. And you've finally found yourself again."

Connor then said he would always be a part of her. He softly kissed the center of her forehead, right above the green stone. The man in the robe smiled and shook Celeste's hand. Celeste found herself a bit perplexed by her surroundings and the mysterious ceremony. She had been enjoying the moment, the calmness, and joy, but now she was compelled to learn more.

"I don't understand," Celeste said. "What is happening here?"

"You're a part of my world now," Connor said. "You can no longer return to the physical world. This is your home."

"Did I die?" Celeste asked. Suddenly images of her running and the car heading toward her flashed through her mind. She felt the impact of the vehicle striking her body like a ton of bricks. Startled and horrified, she let out a piercing scream.

Connor held her tight and stroked her hair. "You're okay," he said. "Everything is all right."

"I died! I'm dead!" Celeste cried. "This can't be happening."

"No," Connor replied. "There is no death. Only a changing of worlds. Your physical body is no longer alive, but you are very much alive and always will be."

"But what about Chip? My poor baby. How will he ever get through this? He just lost his mom!" she sobbed.

"Don't worry," Connor said reassuringly. "Chip will be fine. I've been preparing him for this moment a long time now. He will miss you, of course, but he knows you will visit him sometimes, just like I have."

"What? You mean you knew about this all along?

Why didn't you tell me, Connor?"

"We're not allowed to interfere with predestined events. We can help to support, teach, and guide people on earth. We can protect them from unanticipated events and natural disasters. But we can't stop death when someone's time has come." This actually made sense to Celeste. She stood there quietly, not sure what to say or what was next for her. "How do you feel?" Connor asked. "Are you angry with Andy?"

"Strangely, no," Celeste replied, feeling a bit confused. "I understand the pain and torment he experienced throughout his life. He didn't want to hurt me. He just never learned any other way to relate to people. Violence was how he responded to every emotionally charged situation—positive or negative. He was a victim, too. His father abused him as a child. He led a life filled with pain and self-loathing. So, I guess, in a way, I feel sympathetic toward him."

"You feel sympathy toward the man who abused you and killed you?" Connor asked. "The man who was responsible for my death, as well?"

"Yes. It is odd, isn't it? I mean, I should be fuming mad at him right now. He took your life. He took my life. He took me away from my family. But I'm not mad at all. I forgive him."

Connor smiled with a knowing look on his face. He completely understood how she was feeling. "That's how it is over here," he explained. "Heaven is full of love, peace, understanding, and forgiveness. Hard feelings, grudges, hostility, and hatred just don't exist here."

"That's incredible. What a wonderful way to live!" she exclaimed.

"Yes, it is!"

Celeste became aware once again of the mysterious man in the white robe. He was standing silently in the background, observing them. Her gaze fixed on him. He didn't look anything like God or Jesus to her. But somehow, he seemed important.

"Who is this man? What are we doing here?" Celeste asked.

"This man is Jorge Feliz. He is a master teacher and healer," explained Connor. "His mission is to help souls advance and learn to spread love, joy, healing, peace, and understanding to others."

"You mean, we have jobs here?"

"Sort of. But they're more like our souls' purpose rather than an occupation."

Your soul's purpose is for eternity. Celeste remembered her dream with Star Walker. This must be what she had meant. Suddenly she felt calmer. She smiled warmly at Jorge. "Nice to meet you," she said, extending her hand.

"The pleasure is all mine," Jorge replied as they shook hands.

"So, what was the ceremony you conducted?" Celeste asked.

"It's called 'soul melding.' The process reinforces the connection between two souls and fully merges their energies together," Jorge explained. "It is used for those we identify as complementary forces. By joining them together, they become stronger and can create great change in the world."

"So, Connor and I are like a team now?" she inquired.

"Sort of. It's more like you are two working parts of one system. Your sensitivity, creativity, and cautiousness have combined with his strength, protectiveness, and exploratory nature. Your mutual love and passion has morphed into an endless ball of energetic healing. Together you have become a catalyst for positive change. You and Connor will accomplish miraculous things both in this world and the physical world. Joining forces will allow you to have a big influence over those still living on earth. You will be able to help them understand the world better and enlighten them on how to live more lovingly, peacefully, and harmoniously. You will bring light and love to a world in desperate need of change."

"Sounds like a pretty important job," said Celeste.

"Yes, it is," said Jorge. "We have been waiting a very long time for you and Connor to arrive. We have others already working in similar roles, but your combined energies are the strongest and brightest we've ever encountered. Welcome and congratulations to both of you! Now, I'll leave you to get reacquainted."

Another bright, blazing star appeared. Jorge stepped into it and disappeared. Connor and Celeste stood there facing each other, gazing into each other's eyes. "Connor," Celeste began. "When we first met and you looked at me, I felt like you touched my soul. I feel that again now."

"Me, too," Connor said, with that dazzling, familiar smile. "I feel like we are finally where we're supposed to be. And together, we can accomplish anything."

Celeste returned his smile with her own flirty smirk. As they looked deep into each other's eyes again,

Celeste and Connor felt abundant love, joy, and peace. It was as if nothing else mattered but the powerful magnetic energy they had created. The energy they would bring to the world.

Connor leaned in and passionately kissed Celeste. Every particle of her being vibrated and illuminated, creating a golden glow all around them. It was the most intense and amazing feeling she had ever experienced. She reached up and ran her hands through his wavy, brown hair, returning his kiss with equal warmth and passion. They embraced tightly, their bodies blending together as one. Slowly they spun around, engaging in a slow, melodic dance. A gust of wind swept through them, and they began spinning faster and faster, until they disappeared into a swirling, white mist. All that remained was a glorious, colorful glow that lit up the sky like the northern lights.

❊ ❊ ❊

Chip awoke abruptly. It was still dark outside, although there was a slight hint that morning was approaching. The dream he'd just had was still fresh in his mind. He could still see the image of Mommy. She was glowing, and her hair was longer than usual and very shiny and flowing. She wore a knee-length, white dress with many uneven layers. She looked so pretty! He remembered how she had smiled at him and said: "I love you! Tell Daddy I love him too."

But why didn't she just come into his room and wake him up like she usually did? She had never told him she loved him in a dream before. Where was

Mommy, anyway?

He raced to his parents' bedroom with his little heart pounding. Mommy wasn't there. "Daddy!" he screamed.

***

Dave jumped out of his deep sleep. He had returned to their house just hours after he had taken off his wedding ring and left Celeste for good. He had no intention of getting back together with his wife, but something had told him that Chip needed him. A nagging feeling inside had urged him to go back to their house and check on his son.

When he entered their home, Chip had been sleeping soundly, but he couldn't find Celeste anywhere. He assumed she'd gone off to find Connor again. He didn't understand how she could just leave their son alone like that and was angry with her for putting a small child in danger. He knew he had to stay the night until Celeste returned, so he climbed into bed and fell asleep.

"Chip, what's wrong, buddy?" he asked sleepily.

"Where's Mommy?" he asked, with tears forming in his eyes. Chip already knew the answer. Connor had told him this day was coming.

"I don't know," Dave replied, feeling alarmed. Celeste should have been back by now. It wasn't like her to be gone for so long, especially when she knew Chip was alone. Something wasn't right here. Celeste loved Chip very much and would never just abandon him. He could see the worried look on his son's face and didn't want to frighten him. Thinking quickly, he offered a simple explanation: "Maybe she's in the bathroom. Let's go look for her."

Dave and Chip split up, each taking different sections of the house. They searched every corner of their home, but Celeste was nowhere to be found.

"Dad! Come here! You've got to see this. It's amazing." Dave headed for the family room, where Chip was standing and pointing at the wall. He looked in the direction of Chip's finger. The little bit of moonlight coming through the window cast an unusual shadow on the wall behind the end table. *It couldn't be!* He blinked. He rubbed his eyes and looked again. Sure enough, he saw it, clear as day.

"Dad, it's a lady praying!" Chip said excitedly. "Maybe it's a sign!"

But who could be sending such a sign? From what Dave had come to understand about signs, they usually came from someone who had passed away. Dave wasn't aware of anyone...oh, no! Not Celeste!

The doorbell rang. Dave flung open the door and saw a police officer standing there with a solemn look on his face. Before the man was able to say a word, Dave started sobbing. Chip put his little arm around his dad and cried, too. They both stood in the doorway for several minutes holding each other, their tears flowing freely.

The police officer stood there, unsure of what to do. This family obviously knew what he was about to say. How could he ever possibly console them or make this any easier? Although he was a man of power and authority, he felt powerless. This was by far the hardest part of his job. He liked to protect people, but he couldn't protect them from this.

"It's my wife, isn't it?" Dave said, finally.

"Yes, sir. I'm afraid it is. You wife was hit by a car. She died at the scene. I'm so sorry. The driver admitted that he murdered her. We have him in custody right now, and he will pay for his crime."

"No!" Dave yelled. "How can this be happening?" His sobs turned to the painful, piercing cries of a soul in profound distress. He had just lost the love of his life. What would he do without her?

Dave was also filled with regret. He had run out on her, once again. He had let her down when she really needed him. What had he done? Would she ever forgive him?

"I'm very sorry, sir," the officer said again, patting Dave on the shoulder.

Chip looked up at his father and grabbed his right hand. He gently planted a soft, loving kiss on his father's hand. "Daddy," he said quietly. "Look."

Through his tears, the little boy was staring out the front door into the early morning sky. The sun hadn't quite come up yet, but there was something interesting and mysterious up in the clouds.

Dave gazed into the sky and saw the beautiful, vibrant colors: pink, green, purple, red, and blue. It wasn't a sunrise. It was something different. Something more. Something special. "Wow," Dave said softly. "That looks sort of like the northern lights, but different." The police officer stood watching in amazement, as well. He had never seen anything like this in all his life.

The three of them quietly took in the beauty and

wonder of the sky. The rich, glowing colors that illuminated the lingering darkness mesmerized them. They absorbed the peaceful, loving feelings that were now encircling them.

"It's Mom," Chip said confidently. "I can feel her…and there's more."

"He's with her, isn't he?" Dave said.

"Yes, Connor is with Mom."

"I guess she was meant to be with him all along," Dave said.

"It's okay, Dad," Chip said, gently stroking his hand. "She loves you, too. She told me so."

"She did?"

"Yes, in a dream."

"And what else did she say?"

"Not much. But Connor told me a lot. He said that he and Mom have a special purpose together. It's what they were meant to do. God chose them for a mission. They will be important angels in heaven, and they will help a lot of people on earth."

"I don't doubt that," Dave said, laughing. "Your mom always did have a big heart." Somehow Dave found it in his heart to forgive her. This whole scenario, their broken relationship, the connection with Connor— none of that had been her fault. It was her destiny. No matter what either of them said or did, they could never change what was meant to be.

He would love and miss Celeste for the rest of his life. But he knew she was safe and happy with Connor. They were together at last, and apparently off to bring great things to the world. As hard as it was, Dave knew that some things in life were just written in the stars.

God always has a plan. Celeste and Connor were an integral part of that plan. It wasn't what Dave had wanted or expected, but he had no choice but to accept both his and Celeste's fate.

Dave, Chip, and the police officer watched in silence as the captivating colors that filled the sky slowly dimmed from view, leaving behind echoes of paradise. The echoes would remain in their hearts and form a lasting impression that they would never forget. They had witnessed a precious glimpse into the world beyond, life eternal, and the promise of better things to come. They now knew, beyond a shadow of a doubt, that those who pass are not lost, that humankind is never alone, and that love never really dies.

THE FLIGHT OF THE EAGLE
by Deanna (Aleck) Kahler

The sun shone extra brightly that day
And all seemed right with the world
But it was time for the eagle to leave this place
That he called home
So as the grass became greener
And the flowers began to bloom
He spread his wings and let the gentle breeze
Lift him up into the sky

Although we will not see the eagle
In familiar surroundings again
He will always be with us in spirit
If you listen hard enough,
You can hear his whispers in the wind
If you watch closely,
You will see him soaring high above the earth
Looking down lovingly on all that he left behind

We may long to feel the tender brush of his wings on our skin
But we don't need to reach out to feel his presence
For his love and kindness have touched us all
He has left a little part of himself
With everyone he has ever known
And all the hearts he has ever lifted
So next time you look up into the clouds
Know that he is there
Watching over us all
Seeing sites he had only dreamed of
And waiting until one day
When others will spread their wings and join him
In a paradise like no other

In Loving Memory of Papa,
James C. Aleck
(September 12, 1920–April 5, 1998)

ACKNOWLEDGMENTS

A special and heartfelt thank you goes out to all those who helped with the creation of this book. First, to my husband Paul: Thanks for once again providing constructive criticism. I also appreciate that you were patient with me while I explored what many consider to be a bizarre topic and devoted a lot of time and energy to my own spiritual development.

To my daughter Katie: Thank you for always believing in me and brightening each day with your warmth, compassion, and abundant enthusiasm. I love that you look at the world with an open mind, appreciate the beauty and wonder all around you, and trust your intuition.

To my sister Dawn: I am grateful once again that you gave up some of your free time to proofread my book and offer feedback. I am glad to have a sister who is also my friend.

To my parents: Thanks again for always believing in me no matter what. I know I haven't always been the easiest child to raise and support, but you've been there for me during my lowest points and you never gave up on me—even when I was being stubborn or irrational.

I also wish to acknowledge the following: my editor for the awesome work copy editing this book; the professionals who reviewed *Echoes of Paradise;* and my friends Jessie and Nicole for listening to my unusual experiences with an open mind.

As strange as it sounds, my biggest source of help and inspiration for this book actually came from those who have passed. My acknowledgements would not be complete without crediting the people who have had a positive impact on my life and who are no longer with us on earth. Thank you! I feel blessed to have shared a part of my life and my heart with you!

Finally, thank you to God for all of the incredible blessings in my life and for giving me the strength, determination, and courage to overcome obstacles and pursue my dreams.

ABOUT THE AUTHOR

Award-winning author Deanna Kahler is a passionate professional writer with more than 20 years of experience in corporate communications and advertising. Her work has appeared in numerous  newsletters and magazines and on websites across the country. She began writing as a young child and enjoys the opportunity to reach others and make a difference in their lives.

Echoes of Paradise is her second book. The story is close to her heart because it was inspired by some of her own experiences.

Deanna holds a bachelor's degree in communication arts from Oakland University in Rochester, Michigan, where she graduated with honors. She lives with her husband and daughter in the Detroit area and enjoys writing, dancing, walking, and visiting parks in her spare time.

For more information about the author, please visit www.deannakahler.com.

"Life is eternal;
and love is immortal;
and death is only a horizon;
and a horizon is nothing save
the limit of our sight."
– R.W. Raymond

61082748R00126

Made in the USA
Charleston, SC
11 September 2016